# The White Walls

Lucilla Andrews

WYNDHAM BOOKS

This print edition first published 2021
by Wyndham Books
(Wyndham Media Ltd)
27, Old Gloucester Street, London WC1N 3AX

First published 1954

www.lucillaandrews.com



ISBN: 978-1-915043-00-9

Lucilla Andrews wrote 33 novels, an autobiography, and many serials and short stories. Her books were published in 11 languages and sold almost 3 million copies during her lifetime. *The Nursing Times* said that Lucilla was 'arguably the best of all writers of hospital fiction', and *The Guardian* called her the 'brand leader in hospital fiction'.

Wyndham Books have reissued all of Lucilla's novels and serials as ebooks, and are now publishing paperback editions of these much-loved stories.

Find out more and join the free mailing list for news and special offers at **www.lucillaandrews.com**

# CHAPTER ONE

Sister Margery Oxenham, the Senior Sister Theatre at St. Augustine's Hospital, London, swept into the glove-room of the largest operating theatre early one Monday morning.

I was testing the surgical gloves from the previous day's cases. 'Good morning, Sister.'

Sister was a tall, thin woman, an inch or two taller than myself, with a back like a guardsman's, a firm mouth and two dimples that belied her whenever she attempted to be the autocrat which, according to legend, all senior Sister Theatres at Augustine's eventually became.

'Well, Nurse Maitland?' She stood in the open doorway, her eyes glancing automatically down the neatly numbered shelves. 'Did you enjoy your holiday?'

'Very much, thank you, Sister,' I said, and reached for the pencilled list of the day's cases I had left on the shelf. I compared the written list of names with my mental list of the gloves we would need for the first case. The sterile glove drum was already in the Theatre. 'Two sevens, one eight, and a six-and-a-half for yourself. I suppose you are taking the List as usual, Sister?'

'I am not,' she said firmly.

I looked round quickly in surprise. Sister always took the Monday morning List.

'Have you only been away two weeks, Nurse Maitland? It seems so much longer. I must say,' she added grimly, 'you could not have picked a worse time to buy a trousseau.'

'Why?' I was more surprised now. I had left for my holiday with Sister's complete approval. She knew all about my engagement and why I had wanted the two free weeks, to buy clothes and to haunt the antique shops of the small mid-Sussex town where my parents lived, to look for wonderful bargains for the still more wonderful new home that was shortly to be mine.

She held up her right hand and I saw a neat square of plaster was strapped over the tip of the second finger.

'Sister! You've not had a whitlow?'

'Under the nail,' she said mournfully. 'I had the indignity of having it treated in my own Theatre, three days after you left. I haven't lived it down in the Sisters' Home yet! And, incidentally, I haven't been able to take a case myself since. Which is why I am so thankful to see you back – as I don't doubt Nurse Evans will be when she returns this afternoon! Matron has been very good at sending us reliefs, but all the same, you know what these men are – how they do like to have the staff they're used to, particularly the instrument nurse they are used to! So poor Nurse Evans as my one remaining Staff Nurse has had no proper off-duty since you went away.'

'I see.' I had wondered about Nurse Evans. I had gone up to her room last night when I got back and found she was out. The Theatre Third Year nurse had told me this morning that Nurse Evans had gone home and Sister would be on at eight. That was only half an hour ago, and during that half-hour, one of the busiest – if not the busiest – of the day, the Theatre juniors had been working hard in the Theatre, cleaning, polishing, scrubbing, setting for the day's cases.

As the Senior Staff Nurse, my first chores were the dispensary list and the gloves. There had been no time for any chatting other than 'Hallo, Nurse Maitland, nice to see you back' or 'Did you have a good holiday?' In a big hospital the line dividing the trained staff and the untrained is very marked, and student nurses do not gossip with Staff Nurses. The converse was equally true, and remembering how much I had held in awe the Staff Nurses in my own training days, I understood their reticence.

'So you'll be doing Mr. Hedley's List this morning and Mr. Forbes' this afternoon,' said Sister. 'They are all straightforward cases.' She glanced above her desk to where another list of the day's cases had been pinned by Mr. Hedley's house-surgeon. 'I don't think there's anything else I have to tell you,' she went on. 'Everything else is much as before.'

'Thank you, Sister.'

'Well now –' her voice relaxed – 'and how are the preparations for the wedding going?'

'Beautifully, thank you, Sister.' I beamed at her as I beamed at everyone these days. 'I've bought all I need, and far more than I can afford. The last two weeks have been like a dream. Far too good to be true.' *And the miracle is*, I added to myself, *that it is true.*

Sister said dryly, 'I have noticed Dr. Blake wandering round the hospital in a state of coma. Apparently he feels the same.'

I saw her dimples deepen.

Dr. Blake was William Howard Blake, M.R.C.P., the Medical Registrar. He was also my fiancé. Bill had been in the hospital for ten years, I for five. For the first three years of my training we had not met. In a large teaching hospital it is more easy not to meet, than to meet, a given person. But on the last night of my last spell of night duty as a nurse in training, Bill had walked into the corridor of the surgical ward of which I was temporarily in charge.

I had heard him ask my junior, 'Where's Nurse Maitland?'

I remember how surprised I was that he knew my name, and I remember how the corridor light played on that odd, attractive white streak in his thick, pale brown hair.

I had come out of the kitchen. 'Can I do something for you, Dr. Blake?'

He had smiled suddenly. 'Yes, I think you can, Nurse,' he had said coolly.

I waited and he went on, 'For the past three years, Nurse Maitland, I have been waiting to meet you in some medical ward. You must have done some medicine?' I had nodded, too staggered to answer. 'Well, I can now give the lie to the theory that everything comes to him who waits. You didn't. So I've come to you. What you can do for me is this. You can have dinner with me on your next evening off.'

I had no breath to say anything but, 'Yes, Dr. Blake.'

The third time I dined with Bill, he proposed. The fourth time, I accepted. It had been as simple, as perfect, as that.

When I finished my general training, I had trained as a midwife; then Matron had offered me this job in the Theatre. I had accepted it as a good way in which to fill in the year that must pass before Bill's contract with the hospital terminated. In two months from now that period would be reached and we would leave the hospital behind us. Ahead lay our future, our glorious, unbelievable future. Bill was going into General Practice with his father; we had a house promised.

Sister was speaking again. 'Can you come sufficiently down to earth to run the Theatre for me this morning? Since I'm useless, I thought I might attend that Sisters' lecture at the Royal College.'

I smiled. 'Of course, Sister. Are there any emergencies cooking in the hospital at the moment?'

She said there was one head case that might have to be done. 'I know Mr. Sanders is not anxious to operate on the girl, but he may have no option.'

'Mr. Sanders, Sister?'

'Nurse! Wake up! Mr. Sanders. You know quite well who I mean! Mr. H. J. Sanders. Sir Inister's First Assistant. The brilliant young man who has been in the States these past two years. He's back now – just as well, too.' (Sir Inister MacFallor was the Cranial Surgeon to the hospital.)

'Why, Sister?' I remembered quite well now.

'Sir Inister is poorly. A bad chill which means that of course he can't operate, so it's as well that Mr. Sanders is back.' She thought a moment. 'Mr. Sanders would be before your time in the Theatre, I suppose. You've never worked with him?'

'I haven't,' I said. 'I do know who he is, naturally. I had merely forgotten his name for the moment. I think I would know him by sight, although I'm not certain of that. I remember you've always said he was a first-rate surgeon. What a good thing he's back.'

I had finished my gloves. I moved out of the small room and shut the door. Sister rolled up her sleeves methodically. She said, 'You had better do the needles next,' but as she made no move herself I knew she had more to say and waited by her.

'I'm sorry for that young man,' she said thoughtfully.

'For Mr. Sanders, Sister? I thought you've always said he was the surgeon with the most brilliant future ahead of him.'

'So he has,' she said briskly. 'But that doesn't prevent my feeling sorry for him.'

It was Monday morning and I had a great deal to do, but I was too fascinated to move. 'I don't understand,' I said.

'I should have thought you would have understood, Nurse,' she said calmly. 'I expect you do, when you come to think about it. Life is not concentrated between the four aseptic walls of this Theatre,' she announced. 'Being a success at one's job is a good thing – and one's duty – but it's not everything. And when you are young and shoot to the top, as Mr. Sanders has – he's a Master of Surgery and First Assistant to Sir Inister at thirty-two – you must sometimes wonder what it's all about.'

I gaped.

'Nurse Maitland, it isn't only women who fall in love; it isn't only women who feel lonely,' she said gently. 'Since Mr. Sanders has been back, and since, because of this wretched finger, I've had more time than usual to observe the people in my Theatre, it has seemed to me that he is a lonely man. Remember he's been away two years, and a great deal has happened in the hospital in that time. Most of his contemporaries have gone, and, I suspect, all his friends.' She was quiet for a moment, and her face was sadder than I had ever seen it. 'It's as lonely at the top in hospital as anywhere else, and that young man is discovering the fact.' She smiled briefly and without humour. 'Now for goodness' sake, Nurse, get on with your needles or I won't be at the top a minute longer.'

The morning raced by; the patients came and went; Mr. Hedley's four dressers, which was the name given to the senior students who studied under him, clustered round the table; and the gallery that lined the room but was cut off from the Theatre floor by glass walls, was filled with more students. From there they could see and hear, but could not disturb the surgeons in any way.

Every now and then Mr. Hedley would raise his head. 'Note this, gentlemen!' 'Now, see the condition of this.' 'I use the instruments so!' 'I tie, here.'

At last it was over. Seven cases, four men, three women, had been operated upon. Sister was back from her lecture and saying, 'I'm afraid you'll only have twenty-five minutes for lunch, Nurse. That last case took longer than I expected. What happened?'

'It took longer than Mr. Hedley had expected, too,' I said. 'There was more extensive damage than the X-ray showed.'

Sister said soberly, 'I'm sorry about that. Was Mr. Hedley satisfied when he finished?'

I said I thought so. 'He said "Right" the way he does when he's pleased.'

'That's good. Well, you be off to your lunch, Nurse. It's nearly half-past one now and the list starts again at two.'

I changed quickly, then raced along the corridor to our dining-room. The door of the Doctors' dining-room lay opposite to ours. The door opened as I passed and Bill came out. He had another man with him, a man I did not recognise. I paid little attention to the stranger. I never saw anyone else when Bill was around.

Bill said, 'Why, Clare! I didn't expect to see you at this hour. I thought you went to early lunch on Mondays.' Then he said almost formally, 'This is someone whom I'd like you to meet.' He smiled at the man beside him. 'We shared digs once in the dim past when we were taking our Second M.B. together as student men. Since then he's soared to dizzy surgical heights! Hugh Sanders. Clare Maitland.'

Mr. Sanders was a tall man. I am tall for a woman; even so, I had to look up a long way. His hair was black and his eyes so dark that they seemed black, too. His skin was deeply tanned, as if he were used to a far stronger sun than the rather fitful one that was shining outside on this August day in London. Then I remembered the two years he had just spent in that southern state in the U.S.A.

We shook hands. He said, 'I have to wish you happiness, Miss Maitland – and offer old Bill here my congratulations. That's the correct formula, isn't it?' He had a very slow, deep voice.

I smiled. 'That's perfect, thank you, Mr. Sanders.'

Something made me look at Bill. I was surprised to see he was not smiling now, he was frowning. He noticed my glance and his expression altered. His face closed. It was an extraordinary sensation, as if he had shut a door in my face. I reminded myself happily that Bill would never do that to me. Something Hugh Sanders must have said previously had perhaps upset him. I decided quickly that I did not care for Mr. Sanders.

I would not care for anyone who could upset my Bill.

Mr. Sanders said, 'Will you excuse me? I have to see a patient in Elizabeth Ward.' He did not wait for an answer, but walked quickly away down the long, white, rubber-floored corridor.

Bill looked after his retreating back, almost thoughtfully, then turned slowly to me. 'So you had a good holiday,' he said.

'It was lovely,' I said, 'or as lovely as it could be without you. But, darling –' I was suddenly anxious, Bill was somehow unlike himself this morning – 'I wish you had had a holiday, not me.' I hesitated. 'You look tired.' That was not what I meant, but it was probably the reason. Resident doctors in any hospital are generally tired, despite the fact that they are healthy young men. They work incredibly long hours, and hardly ever have an uninterrupted night's sleep.

'I'm all right,' he said absently. 'I'm sorry I couldn't manage to see you last night. There was a panic in Margaret.' Margaret was the largest women's medical ward in the hospital.

'Darling,' I said again and smiled, 'I'm not a doctor's daughter and a doctor's fiancée for nothing! I know these things just happen!'

'They do,' he said in the same tone. 'Look, Clare –'

'Yes?'

'I have to rush, myself. That woman in Margaret – but when are you off?'

'This evening.' I was right, he was tired. Bill never forgot things, normally. 'Remember I told you on the phone last night?'

He glanced at his watch. 'Look, Clare, I'll ring you.'

'Of course, darling,' I said. 'Any time. You know that.'

He said, 'Yes.'

'And Bill –'

He had begun to move away, he turned back. 'Yes?'

'I saw the most wonderful oak chest in that little shop in the High Street. It would be perfect for the hall. It matches the chairs.'

He hesitated, then all he said was, 'I'll be ringing

you, Clare, and we can talk.'

'Do that,' I said cheerfully and went in to my now very belated lunch. As I sat down I realised that Bill had not gone up the stairs to Margaret, but had turned off at the alcove that sheltered Matron's office from the corridor. What on earth could he want in Matron's office? I smiled contentedly. It did not matter. Whatever Bill did was all right with me; and I thought for the hundred thousandth time how wonderful it was to feel that way about a person; to be able to trust someone; to feel so secure.

When I arrived back fifteen minutes later I found an orgy of cleaning going on in the spotless Theatre. Sister was nowhere to be seen, but Nurse Martin, the second-year nurse, was waiting for me, brimming with information.

'The thoracic list has been cancelled until tomorrow morning, Nurse Maitland. Mr. Sanders is doing an emergency at two-thirty on one of Sir Inister's cases in Elizabeth. Sister has had to go to the office but she told me to tell you, and she left a note for you.'

Nurse Martin handed me the small slip of paper bearing the message in Sister's tidy, upright script. I read the specific name of the case, then went over to the Head cupboard for the necessary instruments. The operation was routine, but an emergency routine as head cases often are.

Nurse Martin knocked again on the open duty-room door.

'I'm so sorry, Nurse, I forgot to give you something else. This letter. Sister Elizabeth brought it in on her way back from lunch. About five minutes ago. She said she had seen you go into the dining-room late and guessed you wouldn't have time to look for your post.'

Sister Elizabeth was Angela Shane, a member of my own now much-depleted set of nurses. Half my set had already left and married. Three were Sisters, five of us Staff Nurses. Angie was one of my best friends; she was one year older than myself, and at twenty-seven the youngest Sister in the hospital. She and I had been friends for years before we came to the hospital. We both lived in the same small town, had both gone to the same school at the top of the High Street. Her father had been the local vicar as mine was the local G.P.

I thought about Angie and how much I was going to miss her when Bill and I had settled in Kent. She would come for visits, of course, and we would love to have her, but I knew things would never be quite the same. I unbuckled my belt automatically and took off my apron, my mind still on Angie.

As my apron bib fell, so did the envelope Nurse Martin had given me and which I had tucked, as all nurses do, into my bib. There was not much time for letter-reading at the moment, even though I had this extra quarter of an hour's grace due to the changing of the afternoon's cases. I knew the letter could not be important. I had left my parents after the last post had gone, last evening. My three brothers never put pen to paper. '*We mean to write, Clare*,' they said as brothers always do, '*but Mummy does it so much better than we could! And, anyway, she gives you all the news*.'

The envelope had fallen face downwards on the floor. I picked it up casually and turned it over. There was no stamp. I recognised Bill's handwriting, even though it was upside-down. My heart turned over.

Dear Bill. How wonderful of him to write me a welcome-back letter. But it was so like Bill. He was always doing little things, inspired little things, like that. This was one letter I would certainly find time to read. I held the envelope carefully, then opened it gently, as if it held something precious inside, something I did not want to lose. I smiled to myself, and gave a grateful thought to Mr. Sanders for giving me this few minutes in which to enjoy Bill's letter. I propped myself on Sister's desk and began to read.

When I had read what he had written once, I read it again. Then I read it a third time. Then I let the letter fall to the floor. I did not move. I felt icy cold. I sat and stared at the small square of white paper. The small scrap of white with the black marks in neat lines. Could anything so insignificant break a heart?

Nurse Martin knocked on the door for the third time. 'Nurse, the porters have just gone up for the patient. Is that all right?'

I was grateful to my years of training. My theatre discipline took over. 'Quite all right, Nurse. I'll be in the Theatre in a minute. Sister wants Nurse Smith to "dirty" again. Will you see to the Anaesthetic Room?'

'Yes, Nurse,' she said uncertainly, then she said, 'Are you feeling well, Nurse Maitland? You've suddenly gone so white. Shall I find Sister for you?'

'No, thanks,' my voice said calmly. 'I'm all right. It was a bit hot in the dining-room. You get on, Nurse. There is no need to bother Sister.'

'Yes, Nurse.' But she still hesitated and her round face was furrowed with anxiety. She ducked suddenly. 'You've dropped your letter, Nurse.'

'Thank you.' I took it from her and pushed it deep into my dress pocket. She gave me another worried look, then went out, quietly closing the door behind her.

I stood up, untied my cap-strings, took off my cap, put on my operating-room turban. I eased it back on my head, then glanced in the mirror to see that no hair was showing. A stranger's face looked back at me. It reminded me of something Bill had once said.

'*You are like a fine pencil drawing, Clare. Every line of you is beautifully restrained. I often think of you as one of those parchment-coloured medieval angels you see in the old Italian paintings. You've that same fair brown hair, light brown skin and hazel eyes. Everything so gently coloured, nothing violent.*'

There was nothing indefinite about my face in the mirror. My eyes looked black, black as that man Sanders' had seemed, and my face was not pale, it was ash-white.

Bill wouldn't know me if he saw me now, I thought. And then I thought, Do I know Bill? Do I know the man who wrote that letter to me? The letter I now knew by heart?

'*Clare*,' he had written, '*I wouldn't hurt you for the world – and yet I'm going to. I have to. My dear, I must ask you to end our engagement. I am sorry, I can't tell you how sorry, to have to say this, after all this time. But I find I have no option. Perhaps I should pretend. But I know you would not want pretence from me.*

'*I have been meaning to tell you this myself, but I couldn't do it. Not to your face. I expect I am a coward, I know I am a coward, but I couldn't do it that way.*

'*I had hoped that perhaps your fortnight at home might clear things in my mind. I had to think, alone. That was why I did not come down last weekend. I wasn't on duty, as I said I was. I'm telling you this now, as you're bound to find it out, and I don't want to hurt you more than I need. And since there is something else you are sure to hear about, perhaps I ought to tell you now what it is.*

'*My dear, I'm desperately sorry, but I find myself in love with someone else. Nothing else would make me write this letter. You know her, although I don't think you know how I feel about her. I'm in love with Sheila Mandin, Clare – and with your forgiveness, I want to ask her to marry me.*'

He had ended with a touch of unconscious irony. He had signed himself, '*Yours, Bill.*'

Sheila Mandin was the Staff Nurse in Margaret Ward.

The gallery was full that afternoon, not only with students; mingled with the tweed jackets were the white coats of the resident doctors, and here and there the occasional black professional jacket of a Consultant. Mr. Sanders worked for over four hours on that one case.

The Theatre was hot, and as the hours passed it grew hotter. It was very quiet. I stood there, handing instruments, threading the needles to the nylon and silk as Mr. Sanders required, keeping an eye on the patient, on Nurse Smith, on the boiling sterilisers, the saline bowls and the hundred and one other things that are part of the responsibility of the nurse 'taking' the case.

Mr. Sanders' strong hands, strong yet delicate in their rubber gloves, moved backwards and forwards from my trolley to the patient. He seemed to know by instinct which instrument to reach for. He never faltered, he never hurried, and then at last he straightened his back and squared his shoulders. I was not in the state of mind to notice anything extraneous to my job, but I did notice the width of his shoulders, and I wondered if he ever did any orthopaedic work. He was the right build for an orthopaedic surgeon. They always seem to be powerful men.

He said, 'That's it. She'll do. She can go back now.'

Later, when the gallery had cleared and the girl patient had gone back to Elizabeth Ward and the Theatre was empty, he sighed wearily.

'It's an odd thing –' he had turned to the house-surgeon who had been assisting him and who was now taking off his gown – 'it's an odd thing,' Mr. Sanders repeated, 'but the more of these I do the more they worry me.'

'I can understand that, sir,' said the house-surgeon solemnly. 'It must have a snowball effect. Even I can see how tricky it all is; how wrong one could be. I can't imagine how the Old Man has stood the strain of it all these years. Every time I leave this Theatre I feel I've a new crop of grey hairs.'

'What do you think about it all, Nurse?' Mr. Sanders walked over to the trolley.

I pulled my gloves off thoughtfully. I said, 'I think it's all rather terrifying, Mr. Sanders. And wonderful. I never understand how anyone can be a surgeon. I know I couldn't!'

'Squeamish?' he said dryly. 'Come now, Nurse, you're used to the work.'

'It's not that,' I said. 'It's more a question of courage.'

'Courage!' His voice deepened in astonishment; and they both stared at me as if I had accused them of something wrong.

I was glad I still wore my mask. Mr. Sanders' faint sarcasm had made me say more than I meant, but now I had said it I was not sorry. That was exactly what I had been thinking. It had been in the back of my mind most of the afternoon. It had kept all other thoughts away. These big cases always moved me a good deal. The strain, the effort, the painstaking care involved, and the terrible responsibility seemed to me overpowering for any man, particularly young men, as surgeons in big hospitals usually are.

I looked from one to the other. 'Yes,' was all I said.

We three were alone in the Theatre at that moment.

Mr. Sanders said quietly, 'Thank you, Nurse. That was very nice of you.'

The houseman walked away, out of the Theatre, and I heard the door of the Surgeons' Room slam.

Mr. Sanders pulled off his cap, pushed back his thick black hair and untied his mask slowly.

'Will you miss all this, Nurse Maitland? Or will it vanish like a dream in the night? A pleasant, interesting interlude? A way of passing the time?'

I thought, 'This is just the beginning. The first question, from a stranger. Then there will be more, dozens, hundreds, from friends. 'Clare, what happened?' 'Clare – what are you going to do about your job? Are you going to stay on?' 'Clare, how awful! After all this time! And to Sheila Mandin of all people!'

I wasn't going to think of Sheila Mandin now. I shut my eyes momentarily. I couldn't close my ears to those imaginary voices. '*Have you heard about Clare Maitland and Bill Blake? My dear – a case of waiting at the church!*' But what did the questions matter? What did anything matter? Now Bill had stopped loving me.

Mr. Sanders' voice was very cool. 'Does it really take all that thought, Nurse Maitland? It was only a simple question.'

'I'm sorry, Mr. Sanders.' I pulled myself together. 'I'm afraid my mind had wandered to –' I thought quickly – 'to your case. Did you use nylon first, or silk? I can't quite remember, and I want to get it straight.'

'Nylon,' he said briefly. Then: 'I'm surprised you worry about such details now. I would have thought all your spare moments would be filled with thoughts of trousseaux and the rest of that paraphernalia.' Years ago Sister Tutor had told us, 'In this hospital we train you to become mechanical in your work, Nurses. Not because we wish you to become machines, or to treat your patients as such; but simply that whatever eventuality may occur, if you are tired, ill, strained, anxious, your professional mind will be able to cope and render you efficient nurses.'

This afternoon I was learning how well Sister Tutor had done her work. My voice said calmly, 'My spare moments on-duty, Mr. Sanders, are not occupied with my personal affairs. Did I have the instruments in the order that you like? Not having taken your cases before, I was not certain that I was doing everything as you wished.'

'You did all right, Nurse,' he said. He smiled swiftly and his whole face changed. 'And I deserve that set-down. I apologise. In fact,' he added seriously, 'I can't tell you how sorry I am to hear the Theatre is losing you. Our loss,' he bowed slightly, 'is Bill Blake's gain.'

'Someone had to be the first person to know,' I thought, 'and now he was more friendly, it might as well be he.' I opened my mouth to explain just as Jenny Evans, my co-Staff Nurse, arrived back from her twenty-four hours off-duty and shot into the Theatre.

'You poor thing!' she said. 'What a return you've had! You must be worn out. Nip off to tea now, and leave the clearing up to me. Sister warned the dining-room that you and Smith would be late for tea, and

I've just rung them again to say you'll be along in five minutes.'

'Thanks,' I said automatically. 'Will you keep an eye on my sharps?' (This was our usual word for scalpels, needles, scissors.) 'I'll see to the rest when I get back from tea.'

'Right.' She smiled up at Mr. Sanders. 'Don't you want any tea, Mr. Sanders? There's some in the Surgeons' Room now.'

He stretched his arms. 'I could do with a cup, Nurse Evans. Bless you.' He picked up one of the shining artery forceps off my trolley. 'Do you know what they call these things in the States?' he asked casually, then smiled again, that quick, attractive smile. 'Snaps.' I've never forgotten the first time I heard a surgeon say to the instrument nurse, "Gee, honey, pass me the snaps"!'

'Not really?' Jenny laughed. 'He didn't really call her "honey" in the theatre, Mr. Sanders?'

'He did.' His face was back to its normal seriousness, but I noticed his eyes were twinkling with amusement. 'Amongst other terms. And a very fine surgeon he was, too. Do you think we should introduce a little levity into Augustinian surgical circles, Nurse Evans?'

'I'd love to hear you do it,' said Jenny honestly. 'But to be truthful, Mr. Sanders, I can't really see you calling Nurse Maitland or myself "honey".'

He shrugged. 'I'm sure you are right,' he said. 'It's not a circumstance I can visualise myself.'

He turned to me, 'Thank you, Nurse,' he said formally and went out to the Surgeons' Room and tea.

'Now run along, Clare,' said Jenny, 'you look all in. Young Martin told me you looked very off colour after lunch.'

I untied my mask which now hung loosely round my neck. 'I'm all right. I've quite enjoyed having to work hard this afternoon.' Enjoy was hardly the word. I had been grateful for my work.

'A fine thing,' said Jenny cheerfully. 'A fine thing, that's what it is, to see a girl who's keen on her job!'

I thought, 'Shall I tell her?' I shelved it. Not now, I was too tired.

'Did you buy some wonderful things?' she asked.

'Wonderful.' It was the easiest way out. 'Jenny, what's Mr. Sanders like with you, when you take his cases?'

I could not have cared less what he was like, but I knew Jenny loved to gossip and the only way to keep her off the subject of my trousseau at that moment would be to discuss another person. Preferably a man.

'Very nice.' She thought it over. 'Very easy. He's so sure.'

I nodded. I had noticed that, too.

'I don't know whether it is because he's experienced, or just plain brilliant, or both,' she went on, 'but I've never worked with any surgeon who filled me with such confidence. Not even Sir Inister –' she lowered her voice – 'although it's heresy to say that if Sister's around. Mr. Sanders is considerate, too,' she added.

'Do you know him well?'

Her eyes danced. 'And what do you mean by that, Nurse Maitland?'

I forced a smile. 'Well, he seemed to relax when you came in just now. I know I've only met him this one afternoon, but he hardly struck me as the matey type. Then you came in, and I thought you must have been friends all your life.'

'We are only Professionally Acquainted,' she said, 'and my dear, shy, gentle Clare, you know you are always out-of-this-world! You never see anyone but your Bill! Not even –' She broke off suddenly and a faint colour covered her cheeks and forehead.

My hands felt ice-cold, the way they had done earlier in the duty-room. I said slowly, 'I don't even see Sheila Mandin?'

My words fell between us like pebbles. The sound echoed round the white walls of the empty Theatre.

Jenny said quickly, too quickly, 'Clare, you know you mustn't take any notice of me. Everyone knows I talk too much! Why can't I keep my big mouth shut?' she chided herself ruefully.

'Look, Jenny,' I said, 'I don't think you do talk too much, but I wish you'd do some talking for me. You're better at it than I am.' I told her my engagement had ended.

'Have you told Bill yet? You haven't had time to answer that note?'

'I haven't,' I said wearily. 'But he knows the answer. He knows I wouldn't want to keep him to something he didn't want himself.'

'You mean you don't love him any more?' She was incredulous.

'Jenny! You can't turn love off like a tap! Of course I love him. The way I feel now I always will,' I whispered. 'But that doesn't make me want him if he doesn't want me. And as I love him, I want him to have what he wants.' I shrugged and tried to keep the bitterness out of my voice. 'Which seems to be Sheila Mandin.'

'But Clare!' I was touched by the genuine concern in her face and voice. Jenny and I had become good friends in this year we had worked together. 'Clare! You can't just give in. Hand over Bill – everything! Without a fight!'

'Can't I? Why not? What good would fighting do?

And, anyway, I'm not the fighting type. I wouldn't know where to start.'

'You mean to say you are going to say "Thank you very much for letting me choose a house, buy a wedding-dress, break my heart?" And hand him back your ring with your love?'

'Why not?' I said again. 'It's his ring. And he's already got my love.' Then I went out to the duty-room to change for tea.

Someone knocked on the duty-room door as I tied my cap-strings under my chin. I called 'Come in' and went on fixing the lace bow in place. It was almost certainly one of the nurses wanting the laundry book. 'It's on the desk, Nurse,' I said over my shoulder. 'Help yourself.'

'Have you second-sight, Nurse?' asked a man's voice. 'Or do you do it by radar?'

I turned quickly. A thickset young man with vivid blue eyes stood smiling at me. He was Mr. Darvie, the new Surgical Registrar, who had worked with Mr. Hedley this morning.

'I'm sorry, Mr. Darvie, I didn't know it was you.'

He shook his head, still smiling. 'You certainly are psychic knowing my name,' he said. 'I'm a stranger in these parts and we've not met before.'

I smiled faintly. 'We were introduced by Mr. Hedley this morning,' I explained. 'I took the List.'

He said nothing for a moment. He just stood there, smiling at me. Then the smile left his face, but still he did not speak.

'Can I do anything for you?' I prompted.

He blinked, oddly, as if he were waking up. 'Yes, of course, Nurse. I left my watch here this morning. I see it sitting there on the desk as you said.'

'Actually I was talking about the laundry book, but I'm glad we've traced the owner of this,' I said, handing him his watch. 'Nurse Martin found it in the Surgeons' Room when she cleared in there, before lunch. If you lose anything in this Theatre,' I explained, 'you'll always find it sitting here on the desk.'

'I will?' His voice had a trace of laughter in it, his slightly staccato way of speaking was very attractive. 'That's good to know.' He made no move to go.

'Will you excuse me, Mr. Darvie,' I said. 'I'm very late for tea as it is.'

'You've not had tea yet? It's gone six o'clock!'

'It's nearer seven. But I still feel lost without my tea. We keep strange hours in this Theatre.'

'You always work here? Why have I not come across you before?'

I said I had been on holiday. Mercifully, he, the one real stranger in the hospital, would not know the reason for my holiday. He stood back for me to pass and we went through the little corridor off which lay all the small rooms connected with the department: the duty-room, Surgeons' room, linen-room, glove-room; at the far end of the corridor lay the big double doors that led into the anaesthetic room which itself led into the Theatre.

'One way and another, Nurse,' he said lightly, 'you and I will be seeing a good deal of each other in the Theatre.'

'Yes.' He was a pleasant, friendly young man, but now I wished he would go and leave me alone.

He grinned. 'That is the best news I've heard since I crossed the river from the rival firm.' He mentioned the name of the large teaching hospital which for centuries has existed in friendly rivalry with Augustine's.

He held open the far door at that moment, the one leading to the outside world of the hospital. As I passed him, something made me glance back, and I saw Mr. Sanders standing watching us in the open doorway of the Surgeons' Room. The expression on his face drew my attention from myself for a brief moment. I remembered what Sister had said about him this morning. She called him lonely. I would have said *remote* was the better word

Bill did not telephone me that night; nor did I ring him. Instead I wrote him a letter; tore it up; wrote another. That one was not any good either. I walked round and round my room.

Before I went to bed I managed the letter to my parents. I asked them not to discuss it with me, but to see to the official side of the break. I even wrote to the elder of my brothers. Then I tried again, but still I could not write the letter to Bill.

I took my ring off the chain I always wore round my neck on duty. Bill had given me the chain as well. I packed it with the ring, my lovely, lovely ring which had made me so happy, and so proud. I sealed the package quickly, picked up my cloak, tidied my capped head, and walked over to the hospital. I would leave the packet with Sam, the Head Night Porter, and an old friend of mine. He would see that it reached Bill safely.

Sam was talking to someone in the Porters' Lodge when I knocked on the glass door. He reached out an arm from his chair at the switchboard and opened the door.

'Oh, it's you, Miss! Won't keep you a moment. Just getting an outside call through for Mr. Sanders.' He fiddled with one of his many rubber plugs, then turned back to me. 'Were you wanting Dr. Blake, Miss? He's in Margaret, I think, but I'll just give the ward a ring and make sure.'

'Don't bother to do that, Sam,' I said quickly. 'I only want to leave this small parcel for him. There's no need to disturb him now.'

I saw that Sam, who was extremely sentimental about inter-hospital romances, was about to remonstrate, so I added, 'We had quite a day in the Theatre today and I want to get to bed early.'

I put the small square packet down beside him. 'This is it. Thanks.'

Hugh Sanders, who had been standing in the corner of the small room leaning against the wall, straightened, took his pipe out of his mouth, said, ''Evening, Nurse Maitland,' as if he had just noticed me. He nodded at the packet. 'I'll give that to Bill, if you like. I'm on my way to Elizabeth in a couple of minutes; I can give it to him later when he gets up to our sitting-room.'

'Thank you, Mr. Sanders.' What else was there to say?

'Any message?' he asked casually. 'Other than your inevitable love?'

I wrapped my cloak more firmly round my shoulders, as if my cloak were my defence.

'No message,' I said. 'Thank you. Good night, Mr. Sanders. Good night, Sam.'

Sam said hopefully, 'Good night, Miss. Shall I just let Dr. Blake know you looked in, like?'

'Really, there's no need to bother Dr. Blake, Sam. I wouldn't want to disturb him when he's busy.' I saw dear old Sam still wasn't happy, so I looked round at Hugh Sanders, almost desperately. 'Perhaps, after all, you would just tell him I say it's all right? He'll understand. Thank you,' I said again.

'Clare says it's all right?'

'Yes.'

Sam nodded to himself, satisfied. He took a great

pride in his position as Head Night Porter and elderly Cupid to the hospital.

Mr. Sanders' eyes creased with amusement as he looked at Sam.

'I hope Blake is as reassured,' he murmured.

'Yes,' I said. 'I hope so, too.'

# CHAPTER TWO

The next morning, before the day's cases started, I talked to Sister Theatre. When I had finished, she suggested I went to see Matron. 'I think Matron would like you to go to her,' she said gently. Matron was so kind that for the first time I came near to weeping. So far, I had not been able to cry. My eyes were hot and dry and weary, my head ached and my heart felt physically heavy, but I had not shed a tear.

Matron said quietly, 'I am sure you are wise, Nurse Maitland. Far better to acknowledge that a mistake has been made now than later. After all, is not that the main purpose of an engagement?' She smiled at me. 'Speaking strictly from the point of view of the hospital, I'm glad we shall not be losing you just yet, Nurse, and I am sure Sister Theatre has said the same.'

I murmured something in gratitude, then said I was afraid I had, at the moment, no plans for my future, and did it matter very much?

Matron became engrossed with a pile of forms on her desk. 'Nurse Maitland,' she said, 'there are times, in all our lives, when it is wiser to make no plans. It's better to keep on with our daily tasks, leaving the future to take care of itself.' She looked up then, and watched me steadily. 'This is one of those times for you. My advice to you now is simply, go on with your work, do it to the best of your ability. Don't force yourself to a sudden decision you may later regret. But remember, Nurse,' her smile was very kind, 'if ever you feel you must have a change – well, come and see me first, and we'll talk it over together.'

A few minutes later I walked slowly away from her office, and thought over what she had said, and how lucky we were in our Matron. She ran the hospital with an iron control and yet she always knew when to relax that control and talk to a nurse as the wise, helpful woman she was.

A voice from behind me broke into my thoughts. 'Good morning, Nurse Maitland! Are you going my way?'

I was quite relieved to see Andrew Darvie. I preferred a stranger to a friend at that moment. 'I'm on my way back to the Theatre, Mr. Darvie.'

'There's a coincidence,' he said. 'So am I! I've a date with my boss and a couple of appendices at ten. Will you be taking them?'

'I expect so.' It was only just after nine, and Sister had not yet decided the morning work when I had left for Matron's office.

'We look like being uncommonly busy today,' he said thoughtfully. 'I'm afraid you'll have had a surfeit of the general surgeons by the time this evening comes.'

'Is Mr. Hedley operating this afternoon? I thought we were reserving that time for Mr. Forbes. Isn't there a chest he wants to do? The one we didn't get yesterday afternoon because of Mr. Sanders.'

He said the chest case was improving so much that Mr. Forbes was going to wait a couple of days. 'The chap may get away with it, we hope. Mr. Forbes has nothing urgent on hand and the general surgical waiting list is bursting at the seams, so Hedley's booked your department.'

'That's good.' I was thinking aloud. I was thinking again how grateful I was for my work, for the hospital, and for the hectic, organised rush that the day was going to become. Once I got back to the Theatre there would be no more time to think of myself. By tonight perhaps I would be too tired for thought. Perhaps. But tomorrow would be another full day. And the day after, and the day after that would be the same.

Andrew Darvie's square face lightened. 'Keen on your work, Nurse? I cannot flatter myself, or my firm, that the sincerity in your tone is there because of us.'

I had forgotten he was there. I smiled back, absently. 'I like being busy,' I said apologetically.

He said, more seriously, 'You don't have to take me too seriously, Nurse Maitland. There's no call to apologise, certainly to me. And I know what you mean about being busy. I find it the same myself. If there's anything I hate, it's wondering what it is I have to do next. Not a thing that often happens,' he smiled as we walked along. 'The usual form is I have so many things I must do next that, far from wondering, the lot are engraved on my heart. It's a hard life we live in hospitals!'

I glanced at him and saw he had forgotten me much as I had forgotten him a few moments ago. He was chatting it out with himself, and I wondered casually what it was that, like myself, Andrew Darvie wanted to forget.

We had reached the great Middle Hall of the hospital. At that moment, Hugh Sanders came down the last flight of the wide stone staircase that opened into the Hall.

He nodded, unsmilingly. '’Morning, Nurse. ’Morning Darvie.’ Then he stopped, ‘Oh, Nurse Maitland!’

Something in his tone reminded me that although he might be an old friend of Bill, and was still a young man himself, he was nevertheless, a senior member of the hospital staff.

I stopped automatically. ‘Yes, Mr. Sanders?’

He looked faintly amused, as if he had realised why I had answered so quickly.

‘Nothing special. Merely that I delivered your packet and message to Bill Blake last night. I thought you would like to know.’

I opened my mouth to say thank you, but I could not make any sound come. And I could not move. His casual words had somehow made me understand what I had done – I had let Bill go. It was all over.

I stood, foolishly still in the Middle Hall, and the two doctors watched me. Andrew Darvie seemed strangely concerned. Hugh Sanders wore that same expression of cool amusement.

But at that moment the Theatre, my sanctuary, came to my rescue in the persons of Sir Inister MacFallor and Mr. Hedley. The two Consultants had walked in through the main doorway at that moment, and both Mr. Darvie and Mr. Sanders were forced by hospital etiquette to leave me and greet their chiefs. I slipped away, unnoticed, and reached the Theatre duty-room before my held-back tears started.

Sister was busy in the Anaesthetic Room and I wept in private, and then my face, which in any other job would have given me away, was hidden behind a mask for the rest of the day.

***

The weather turned cold and grey the way it often does at the end of an English summer, and although it was only the first week of September, there was a touch of winter in the early morning air.

One Friday morning, three weeks after my return from holiday, and what seemed like three hundred years since my engagement to Bill Blake had ended, Jenny and I shivered as we left the warmth of the Nurses' Home and walked through the grounds of the hospital to breakfast. Jenny pulled her cloak more tightly round her shoulders.

'The year's dying early this year,' she said. 'I can't wait to get to our nice centrally-heated Theatre! Do you remember this time last year, Clare? It was still burning midsummer.'

'So it was!' I pretended the idea had just struck me. The weather was another of the things to which I was eternally grateful these days. It did not remind me, as the calendar did, that it was this time last year Bill and I filled in the long, warm evenings planning our home, scanning house-agents' advertisements, making long, exciting lists.

Jenny and I did not talk much over breakfast, and as I sipped my coffee and played with the roll and butter which was all I was able to manage for breakfast these days, I thought how much I owed to my job now. The Theatre was the one place in the hospital where I ran no chance of meeting Bill, a physician. And since we Theatre staff kept different hours from the rest of the hospital, I was spared the occasional encounter with Sheila Mandin at the Staff-Nurses' table.

'You finished, Clare?' Jenny stood up. 'Or, rather, have you started?'

I stood up, too, and pushed back my chair. 'Thanks,'

I said. 'I'm ready.'

As we hung our cloaks on the pegs in the duty-room, Jenny said suddenly, 'Are you going to the dance tonight, Clare?'

'Dance?' I echoed vaguely. 'Is there a dance?'

'Clare, wake up!' She sounded almost impatient. 'Of course there's a dance! The Rugger Club's fund-raising ball! The whole place has been agog with it all the week, the way it always is. Mike Gill has asked me, and I've been wondering about you?'

I smiled faintly. 'No call to wonder. I'm not going. No one's asked me.'

She frowned. 'Do you want to go?'

'Not particularly.' I thought it over. 'No, I don't think I do.'

'Why not?'

I shrugged. 'Usual reason,' I said at last.

'Bill Blake?'

I shrugged again. 'Yes.' I took off my cuffs and rolled up my sleeves.

Jenny was smaller than I was, shorter, wiser, firmer. 'Hadn't you better be your age, Clare,' she said slowly. 'Your engagement's over. It was bad luck, but it's over. Don't you think it's time you started again?'

'Everyone's always telling me to be my age these days,' I said. 'Angie never stops. Is twenty-six so old? And why should I start again? If you burn your hand in a fire you don't necessarily shove the other hand in to burn it, too.'

'But you can't just retire into the Theatre,' she said. 'Hide yourself behind a mask – turn into another Oxenham! Anyway, Augustine's doesn't need another Oxenham yet. She can't be more than forty. She's good for another twenty years in the old place.'

'There are other hospitals,' I said mildly. 'There are even other Theatres in this one! And, anyway, what's wrong with Sister? You couldn't find a better one anywhere.' I opened the glove-room door. 'I'll see to these, if you like to keep an eye on the nurses in there –' I nodded towards the Theatre – 'and the dispensary.'

'Right' She pinned her watch in her bib pocket 'There's nothing wrong with Sister,' she said. 'Only would you like to be her, in twenty years' time? With this nice aseptic department for a home?'

'This is a far cry from the Rugger dance,' I said. 'Too far for me. I ... want to get on with my gloves.'

She still lingered. 'I wish you were coming to the dance,' she said again.

'I can hardly gate-crash alone – and as I've said, I haven't been asked.'

'I'm not really surprised at that,' she said. 'The men who know you well know all about Bill and don't like to butt in. And the ones that don't – like Andrew Darvie – are far too scared of you to suggest anything so frivolous as dancing.'

'Mr. Darvie? Scared of *me*!'

I had seen a good deal of Andrew Darvie at work during the past three weeks. I had always found him as polite, amusing and quietly friendly as on that first day.

Jenny said, 'Yes. I'll get on with my work in a minute, Clare, but I must finish what I'm saying. You can have no idea just what a touch-me-not air you've got these days. You never had it before. Before you were engaged, I mean, when you were training. It's something that's cropped up since your break-up. That's why the men who know you understand and are leaving you alone. But to a stranger, it shows a completely new, and false, you. I know Andy Darvie thinks you are attractive,' she said quickly. 'I know because Mike told me. And Mike said that Andy thinks you're quite unapproachable.'

To get away from the subject of myself, I said, 'I didn't know you and Mike Gill were on these terms. How long has this been going on? And are you thinking of getting engaged?'

Mike Gill was another Surgical Registrar. There were four others in the hospital, including Mr. Darvie.

'We are good friends.' She laughed. 'It's rather fun! No strings, at the moment, just fun.' She saw me glance at the clock. 'Yes, I'll get on and see to the nurses before you chase me out!'

I thought over Jenny's pep-talk at intervals during the morning. Sister's finger was well again and she took the general surgery that morning. Jenny was in charge of the Ear, Nose and Throat cases that were being done in our annexe. This was a small Theatre attached to our own large one and staffed by the same nurses. It had no gallery, but apart from that was as perfectly equipped as the other.

My job that morning was mainly clerical, with some general overseeing and traffic directing thrown in. Bows and Jones, the two Theatre porters on duty, brought the patients from the wards to the Anaesthetic Room, and then later back to the wards again. One of my jobs was to telephone each ward a few minutes before the porters left for a respective case, to warn them that we were ready for their next case, or conversely, returning one.

Nurse Martin, the second year student nurse, was Anaesthetic Nurse for the morning which meant I would have little to worry about in her department. She was a very bright twenty-year-old, who had taken to Theatre-work like the proverbial duck to water. Sister had already privately marked her down as a future Staff Nurse, when her training came to an end.

As I had expected, Nurse Martin had everything organised. The patient was now sleeping peacefully, and the anaesthetist was fiddling with the closed-circuit apparatus on one of his many trolleys. Nurse Martin was standing by the patient, holding one of the sleeping woman's hands in both of hers.

'All well?' I murmured.

The Resident Anaesthetist raised an eyebrow. 'All serene, Nurse.'

Nurse Martin said, 'Yes, thank you, Nurse. Is the next patient coming down?'

'The porters have just gone up for her,' I said and shut the door quietly behind me.

Nurse Smith, who was 'dirtying' for Sister, came swiftly into the corridor from the Theatre.

'Oh, Nurse Maitland, I was just coming to find you. Mr. Darvie has cut his finger. Mr. Hedley wants him to have some A.T.S., some A.G.G.S. and Penicillin. At once. Sister says please will you see to it?'

'Of course. Is he coming out here?' I had barely spoken the words when Andrew Darvie appeared behind her. One of his hands was bare of its rubber glove and half wrapped in a sterile towel.

'You go back, Nurse Smith,' I said. 'Thanks.' I turned to him. 'Poor Mr. Darvie. I hope you haven't hurt yourself badly?'

'Am I not a fool?' he said cheerfully. 'I cut my own finger when we were stitching up just now.'

'Had you finished?' I asked, hoping that the answer would be yes. It made a lot of difference to how much danger he was running.

He shook his head soberly.

'Not quite. The last lap, but still, there's no getting away from it, my hand was inside.'

I led the way swiftly into the duty-room and moved a chair to beside the hand-basin. 'Would you sit here, Mr. Darvie?'

I poured some hydrogen peroxide into a small bowl, mixed it with boiling water. 'Just let your hand soak in that for a while, and I'll get the injections ready. I won't be a minute.'

'That's what I'm afraid of,' he said ruefully, and pulled down his mask with his good hand. 'I may as well remove my yashmak.' He grinned up at me as I took the small ampoules of Anti-Tetanus and Anti-Gas-Gangrene serum from the cupboard. 'Tell me when to shut my eyes, Nurse Maitland.'

'I will,' I promised as I moved his bowl slightly. 'I'd better put that on the ledge. I don't want to splash it when I wash my hands. But first. I'll roll up your other sleeve.'

'Oh, you needn't bother, Nurse. I can manage.' He took his injured hand out of the peroxide.

'Mr. Darvie,' I said sternly, 'put that back in the lotion at once and leave it to me.'

'You're a hard woman!' he mocked and did as I said.

'Ready?' I asked a few minutes later.

'My teeth are so gritted they are all but worn away!' He watched me empty the syringe twice. 'That the lot, Nurse?'

'Bar the penicillin. I'll have that in a moment It's in the fridge in the other room.'

'I'm afraid I'm giving you a lot of trouble, Nurse Maitland,' he said, more seriously. 'I'm exceedingly sorry. I know how busy you girls always are.'

I said truthfully, 'I'm not all that busy this morning. In fact this is roughly what I'm here for.'

'Succouring the sick Theatre staff?' he asked cautiously. 'Don't tell me that's your work. I thought your life was dedicated to your instrument trolley?' He spoke casually but his eyes were watching me carefully.

'No.' I rinsed out the syringe and put it down in a receiver. 'No. My job isn't only in there.' I jerked my head towards the glass peep-hole. 'I'm a nurse first, an instrument nurse second. So my job is anything from a cut finger to a roaring pneumonia. The fact that you're a doctor on the staff doesn't make you any less my job, if you've hurt yourself and need attention.'

He grimaced. 'You really feel that, don't you, Nurse Maitland?'

I said, 'Yes.' I was suddenly self-conscious and glad of an excuse to leave him. 'Now I'll just get that penicillin.'

He said, 'Don't look so worried. You know, that's not at all a bad way to feel.'

There was something in his expression, something in his voice that I did not understand; something, that I was not sure I wanted to understand, so all I said was, 'I won't keep you long, Mr. Darvie. Excuse me,' and went out in to the small connecting corridor.

Nurse Smith opened the Theatre door as I passed, 'Oh, Nurse Maitland!'

'Yes, Nurse?'

'Sister says would you please ask Florence to keep their patient another ten minutes; she says the porters can wait up there, and then would you ring Mr. Cardray and tell him Mr. Darvie won't be able to go on this morning and would he come down and take his place assisting.'

I nodded. 'Mr. Darvie won't like it,' I said. 'Does he know he's got to stop? I think he imagines he can go on when he's been patched up.'

Nurse Smith said Mr. Hedley said no. 'The next patient is a case with some infection and Mr. Hedley doesn't want Mr. Darvie to run any further risk today. He says would you explain?'

I smiled. 'I don't suppose it'll be easy, but I'll try. And yes, I'll see to the other things at once.'

I did not want to go back to the duty-room to telephone until I had explained things to Andrew Darvie, so I went into the empty Surgeons' Room. Beyond the alcove, where the men changed, was a glass-partitioned booth. I did the telephoning.

Mr. Cardray, the Senior House-Surgeon, was in the middle of a vast out-patients' clinic, but said yes, of course, he would be down.

The porters had just arrived in Florence Ward. It took them over ten minutes to reach the ward from the Theatre. Augustine's is a big place and covers a lot of ground. Sister Florence said she quite understood, and her next patient had not been disturbed yet so she would keep the porters for ten minutes. 'I expect they can do with a cup of something, and Nurse is doing the morning drinks now.'

I put down the telephone and was just going to pull back the curtains that divided the booth from the room when I realised someone had come in. I hesitated, in case Mr. Cardray had arrived and was changing into his operating clothes. Then I recognised two voices talking and neither of the voices belonged to Mr. Cardray. One was Mike Gill, and the man he was speaking to was Tom Friston, the Ear, Nose and Throat Registrar. Mike asked, 'You finished already, Tom?'

'No. Half-time. The boss wants a ten-minute breather, so I thought it worth getting dirty and coming out here for a change of scene.'

Mike asked who was taking the Ear, Nose and Throat List.

'Jenny Evans.'

'Is she still scrubbed-up?'

'Yes. Why? Want her for anything?'

'Give her a message for me, will you, Tom? Tell her I've got to dash over to the other side of the City to see one of Sir Inister's specials. Hugh Sanders and I are off now. This is a big operation, so I doubt if we'll be out before seven. The Old Man reckons it'll take five hours, which is going to break into my dinner-date. So would you tell Jenny why I've vanished and that I'll ring her later? She'll understand.'

Tom Friston said, 'Understanding type, eh, your Nurse Evans? Right. I'll tell her.'

I heard movements and hoped they had gone, when Mike spoke again. 'I wanted to collect my own gown and cap. Can't bear operating in other people's clothes. Doesn't worry old Hugh. So long as he's got a scalpel in his hands, the world can fall in.' I heard them laugh, quietly. Mike went on, 'I was dreadfully afraid I'd run into the Fair Clare. I wouldn't have dared to give her such a frivolous message, and poor Jenny would have had to think I was standing her up!'

Tom Friston said languidly, 'What's wrong with Clare Maitland? She's never been exactly the life and soul of the hospital, but I always thought she was a pleasant, quiet soul.'

'She used to be, you mean,' said Mike. 'She's too busy looking forlorn these days to have time to smile. She makes me feel about two inches high – and unshaven at that! I agree, she was a pleasant girl once. In her own way, she could be a lot of fun. She had quite a sense of humour. Never known a girl to change so!'

Tom's slow voice was casual.

'Taken that bust-up with Bill Blake badly, has she? I wondered what was wrong. I have noticed it, now you mention it. She is different.'

'Different!' said Mike. 'It's knocked her flat. Which is odd. I would have said she had more courage than to wear her willows quite so blatantly. Just shows, you never can tell. Well –' I heard the click of a suitcase shutting – 'that's the lot. Thanks, Tom.'

'O.K.,' said Tom. 'I'll tell Jenny. Better get back myself now.'

There was silence. I stood behind the closed curtain and felt ashamed, hurt, humiliated and finally angry.

How dared Mike talk about me that way! Mike, whom I had always thought such a nice, kindly young man! How dared he! I had thought Mike liked me; that he was my friend. And then I thought, more calmly, perhaps he had liked me. Before.

I walked mechanically in to the Anaesthetic Room. I said the right things to Nurse Martin, opened the fridge, took out the right penicillin, still thinking over Mike's words.

That young men discussed girls as much as girls discussed young men, I already knew. My three brothers have taught me just how much young men do talk! Mentally, I defended my brothers; they were never malicious. A nasty thought pushed its way to the front of my mind. Had Mike Gill been malicious? Or merely honest?

I had to go back to the duty-room and there was no more time for my own little problems, so I ignored the thought. Not very successfully; I knew it was there and the knowledge was not a pleasant sensation.

'Enter Third Torturer,' said Andrew Darvie cheerfully. 'But I'm glad to see you. I was afraid you had got lost in the outer darkness of the Surgeons' Room. I never realised you kept a fridge in there? Quaint ways you have in this hospital!'

'We don't,' I said. 'I had to telephone.' I told him all I had to tell him. 'I'm sorry, Mr. Darvie,' I said, when I had finished. 'I'm afraid Mr. Hedley won't let you operate any more today.'

'He won't, eh?' I noticed absently that Mr. Darvie's jaw was very square as he spoke. He saw me looking at him and his expression relaxed. 'Don't look so frightened, Nurse Maitland. I don't bite, even if I am a bit put out over a microscopic scratch. It was my own fault. There's no point in getting worked up over one's own mistakes!'

'I had better put a small dressing on that microscopic scratch now, Mr. Darvie.' I rinsed out the last syringe and left it in the receiver. 'I've finished all the injections for the moment. But I understand Mr. Hedley wants you to have the usual course of penicillin for the next few days. Will you get the stuff from the dispensary and give it to yourself, go to the Casualty for it, or have it here?'

He stood up and unrolled his sleeve. 'Have I really the choice, Nurse?'

I was washing my hands; I looked over my shoulder. 'Yes. We reckon to do that sort of thing for the surgical staff, but there's no reason at all why you shouldn't have it done elsewhere, if you prefer it that way.'

He said, 'I'd as soon come here. If I must have a needle stuck into me twice a day, I'd rather it was shoved in by you. You've a neat hand with a hypodermic, Nurse Maitland.'

'Thank you,' I said more dryly than I could have wished. I was thinking about Mike Gill. And Bill. I was glad to be good at something.

'I meant that,' he said quietly.

I glanced up quickly. His normally good-humoured face was frowning. 'I'm sorry, Mr. Darvie. I didn't mean to snap. You just interrupted a private thought that had no business to intrude at this moment. Is your hand comfortable?'

'Fine. Thanks.' He took off his Theatre cap and pushed his hand through his hair. 'Ah, well. Maybe I had better shed these pretty clothes and get back into my smooth suiting!' He grinned. 'I'll have to think up a way to use my gratuitous holiday.'

'Catch up on your notes?' I suggested.

'That's the idea.' He nodded, then he said slowly, 'Tell me, Nurse, if it's not an impertinence – which it probably is – do you never think of anything unconnected with work?'

It was just a casual question from a casual stranger, but I felt my face flame to scarlet.

'I'm sorry,' he said more quickly. 'Was I intruding again?'

I shook my head. 'Not at all.'

He obviously did not believe me. He had stopped in the open doorway. 'I've a feeling I have said this before, but you don't have to take me seriously, Nurse Maitland.' His voice was surprisingly kind. 'I'll push off now.' But he did not move. 'I suppose,' he said, then hesitated and smiled swiftly. 'No. I suppose not.'

'What, Mr. Darvie?'

He shook his head. 'We'll let it pass.'

The door leading to the hospital corridor swung back and Mr. Cardray, the Senior House-Surgeon, rushed in.

'Mr. Hedley in the Theatre now, Nurse Maitland? Right. I'll change in a jiffy!' He shook a fist at Andrew Darvie and vanished into the Surgeons' Room.

'You were saying, Mr. Darvie?'

'I was not really saying anything, Nurse. I was thinking aloud. A dangerous habit I have.'

'Oh! I see.' I moved towards the desk.

He said, 'Don't freeze up, Nurse. Can't you go on thinking I'm a patient? You'll forgive me for telling you that you're a different person when you're dealing with a patient. And, after all, you are going to give me my penicillin. So do please forgive me again, if I'm speaking out of turn, but I was wondering about tonight.'

'What about tonight?' It was not intentional, but my voice was icy.

'We-ell –' he hesitated again, then shrugged his shoulders – 'you can but say no! And I've a nasty feeling you'll do just that! But if you're free tonight – not on call or on duty or anything – and you are not going to the Rugger dance with anyone else, I would be very pleased if you would come with me.'

I said nothing, and he went on quickly, 'I know it's awfully late to ask you, and I hope you're not offended by that, but you know, this is really the first chance I've had to talk to you about anything but which instrument I want to use next. So, do you think you could? Please?'

It was very kind of Andrew Darvie to give me so many good excuses for refusing his invitation. I had only to say I was 'on call' for emergencies tonight and he, being a surgeon, would know I could not possibly be free to go to the dance. He would have no means of guessing that it was Sister's night on. These things were arranged between Sister and her two Staff Nurses only.

I thought, 'How can I go with him?' I never felt less like dancing in my life; nor less like facing the eyes of the whole hospital for the first time without

Bill as a partner. And then I thought, 'Bill will almost certainly be there himself with Sheila.' Bill loved dancing. I knew I could not do it.

Mr. Darvie said gently, 'It was just an idea I had. Maybe it wasn't such a good one from your point of view. Never mind.'

He moved slowly away down the corridor towards the Surgeons' Room. His hand was on the door-knob when I remembered Mike Gill's words. '*I would have said she had more courage than to wear her willows so blatantly!*'

'Mr. Darvie.' He spun round. 'Thank you very much,' I said. 'I'm sorry to have taken all this time to answer. I was –' I hesitated – 'I was working out the "on call" list. I am free and I'm not booked. I should like to go to the Rugger dance with you.'

He said nothing for a moment. He stood there and smiled at me, and the way he smiled made me suddenly ashamed of myself.

'How about dinner first? Are you off in time for that?'

I nodded, my mind made up. 'I'm off at six tonight.'

'Will seven give you time to change?'

'Seven will be grand, thanks.' And I tried to sound as if I meant it.

# CHAPTER THREE

The Ear, Nose, and Throat List finished early that morning and Jenny went to first lunch. She came into the duty-room on her return, as Sister and I were filling in the log for the day's cases in the report-book.

'You'd better order some more nylon from the stores in the morning, Nurse Maitland,' Sister was saying, 'or we may run short if we have many emergencies tonight.' She looked up and saw Jenny waiting. 'Were you wanting something, Nurse Evans?'

Jenny coloured faintly, 'I wanted to ask a favour, please, Sister.'

'Well?' said Sister calmly.

'Do you think I could possibly go off an hour early tonight? At seven-thirty? I'm sorry not to have asked earlier.'

Sister's eyebrows drew together. 'We have nothing scheduled after six.' She glanced at the list on the wall. 'But of course that doesn't mean we won't be working. And I dislike leaving the Theatre without a Staff Nurse when I'm away at my own supper.'

Sister Theatre had very few fads, but one of these few was her dislike of any alteration in the off-duty as planned by her each week. Jenny gazed at me hopefully. Sister saw her expression, and smiled. ‘Do you want Nurse Maitland to change with you? Is that it?’

‘Would you, Nurse Maitland?’ asked Jenny formally.

Sister noticed my hesitation and answered for me. ‘Perhaps Nurse Maitland is also disposed to trip the light fantastic! Are you going to the dance, too, Nurse?’

‘Well, yes, I am, Sister,’ I said slowly, and saw Jenny’s look of surprise. ‘But I was wondering if we couldn’t arrange something as we both want to be off?’

I had had no chance to talk to Jenny since early this morning. I was quite amused to see the effect my words had had on her. She could hardly have looked more staggered if I had said I had been made Matron.

‘I appear to be blessed with a very social pair of Staff Nurses,’ murmured Sister. ‘I see we will have to put our heads together.’

She counted the afternoon’s cases. ‘Five straightforward patients. Judging purely from what’s written here, that should take us straight through to six o’clock.’ She thought for a moment. ‘I think the best plan is for Nurse Evans to take my off-duty this evening. I will come back from six to nine – I fancy it won’t harm me to miss supper for one night, and you two nurses work straight through the afternoon and miss tea. Nurse Maitland, take the cases, and Nurse Evans, do my job out here. Now,’ she said firmly, ‘does that suit you both?’

‘Very well, Sister,’ I said. ‘Thank you.’

‘Thank you very much, Sister,’ echoed Jenny.

‘That was decent of the old girl, Clare,’ whispered Jenny as I went to change. ‘I never thought I’d get away with it! It’s your coming that’s worked the trick! Sister’s got a soft spot for you. But Clare – are you going to the dance? And who with? I thought you said –'

'I've changed my mind,' I said severely. 'A woman's privilege. Any complaints, Jenny?'

'You've changed more than your mind.' She tied my belt tapes for me. 'You even look different. What's happened since this morning?'

'I've taken your lecture to heart,' I said.

'But, Clare –' her eyes were very worried – 'who are you going with? Not Bill?'

'Not Bill,' I said flatly. I was suddenly exhausted by it all. 'Andrew Darvie. He wasn't as scared of me as you thought.' I couldn't resist that crack. 'Why? Do you object? I thought that was what you wanted?'

'Clare –' she sounded upset – 'I didn't mean to hurt your feelings!'

'You didn't.' I pulled on my gloves. 'You didn't.' I tried not to accentuate the word *you*.

There was one corner of the large, built-in hanging cupboard in my room into which I now never looked. Hanging there were three dresses. Two of them had been bought on my last holiday. The third I had been making myself. It was unfinished. It was made of white tulle. The slip alone had cost nearly one month's salary. I had always dreamed of a wedding dress in heavy white satin. Bill had insisted 'something soft'; so I had compromised. The dress had not been touched since that last evening of my holiday when I had been tucking the bodice. I had to move the cloud of tissue paper that covered this to reach the evening dress I was seeking.

Bill and I had chosen that evening dress together. It was dark bottle green, a shade so dark as to be almost black, and it had a halter neckline.

I have hazel eyes, which in some lights and with some colours can turn to emerald. More often, as my brothers have told me, they are plain muddy-brown. The colour of that evening dress was the perfect colour for them. I had vowed to myself that I would never wear any of those three dresses. Now I took the green one out deliberately, and shook out the skirt. It was uncrumpled, perfect.

I shuddered. I couldn't wear it. I couldn't bear to wear it! I sat down on the side of my bed and wept all over the skirt. Then I pulled myself together, stood up, decided it would have to be ironed, after all. I went and booked an iron in the washing-room at the end of the corridor.

Angie Shane came out of the bathroom a few minutes later, her hair a mass of rollers, her face ghastly under an oatmeal face pack. She glanced casually through the open door, saw who it was ironing and stopped dead. 'Clare! What are you doing?'

I half smiled. 'Ironing.'

'But –' She stopped the words, swallowed, then said, 'Who?'

'Andrew Darvie,' I said. 'That's who!' Then I smiled properly. 'I think I'll stick a printed form on my forehead. 'I am going to the dance with the new Surgical Registrar.' Surely he's eminently suitable, since I'm a Theatre girl?'

'Eminently,' she said carefully, her smile uncertain. 'I am awfully glad, Clare.'

I put the iron down on the asbestos mat. 'Well, I'm not.' I dropped all pretence. 'I'm scared stiff. And dreading it.'

Angie knew me better than anyone else in the hospital. 'You needn't dread it too much,' she said kindly. 'I don't think Bill will be there.'

'Why not?'

She sighed. 'There's a little girl in Margaret. Meningitis. The physicians are worried about her, I know. That's why I don't think the medical side will be doing much dancing tonight. Dr. Franks is away for the weekend. He went this afternoon before the poor child came in. So that means Bill is in charge, and whatever I may think of that young man's private life, I must admit that as a doctor they don't come more conscientious.' She shook her head. 'An odd combination, Bill Blake.'

Even now, when it was all over, I could still feel a glow when someone praised Bill's work. Then I realised what we were talking about. 'How is that child now, Angie?'

Angie shrugged. 'Sister Margaret wasn't too happy at tea.'

I forgot all about the dance and my own silly, superficial little problems. 'Which type is it?'

Angie told me the type, soberly. 'Still, they've given her a good shot of the stuff.' She mentioned the now usual injections for those cases. 'Too early yet to say if they've taken a hold. But they are plugging it in. She should do.'

'How old is she?'

'Twelve.'

We looked at each other in silence, then she went back to her room. I went on with my ironing, but I did not see my dress at all. I thought of the little girl. I wondered about her parents; if she had brothers and sisters? The more I thought, the more ashamed I felt of myself and the way I had become so wrapped in my own concerns that I had forgotten the hospital and the real tragedy that was going on around me all the time and was the hospital's daily routine.

But if the injections worked, and they so often did, then the child would be saved.

I thought of the joy, the relief her parents would feel tomorrow morning, the weight that would roll from Bill's thin shoulders, and the way he would say: 'Good. Very good. Oh, very, very good, Clare!' And as I thought of that happiness, for once the fact that he would not be saying it to me did not hurt.

No. Tragedy was not the only thing that went on in hospital. It was there, but it was only a part of the whole.

Someone had once said, 'If you have not known real sorrow, how can you know real happiness?'

Oh, how I hoped the little girl's parents would know that happiness. And I knew now that I would watch all night and long to see Bill come in to the dance, because if Bill came in, then that child would be pulling through.

Andrew Darvie was punctual. He told me he had booked a table for dinner, mentioning a well-known restaurant. 'I hope you're not thoroughly bored with the place? Being a stranger in these parts, I wouldn't know. But we can easily go somewhere else.'

'I'm not at all bored with the prospect,' I said. 'In fact, I'm delighted. I've never been there.'

'You've not? That's grand.' He looked keenly at my face. 'But there's something wrong, all the same. What is it?'

'Well,' I said slowly and wondered if I should mention it, 'isn't it a shade expensive?' The moment the words were out I wished them back.

'Miss Maitland,' he said severely, 'I may come from the wrong side of the border, from your point of view, but I have my pride, woman!'

'I'm sorry, Mr. Darvie,' I said meekly and he

laughed.

'Don't look so frightened! It's not serious. I'm only a trifle offended!'

We went out to the waiting taxi. Bill was fairly well off. He had a small income of his own apart from what he earned; all the same, a home takes a lot of money, and for months past we had been careful, he and I, going only to small cafes, taking a bus or walking to save petrol and wear and tear on his car. Bill used to joke. 'A car is as essential to a good G.P. as a wife, darling. I've got to take care of the two of you!'

Of course, this was different. This was merely an odd evening out with a single man, without ties or obligations. And then, while Andrew was directing the taximan, I thought, 'How do I know that? I know nothing of him, except as a surgeon, or he of me, as a Theatre nurse.' And for no reason at all my mind strayed to Hugh Sanders as it had done once before, and I wondered again what he was like, away from the bright lights of the Theatre.

We had a pleasant meal. Andrew Darvie talked well and very amusingly, and I found myself laughing a lot. Even so, the meal seemed to me endless. But at last he beckoned the waiter for the bill.

'I suppose we should be getting back,' he said almost regretfully.

I sat back in my chair. 'Don't you care for dancing, Mr. Darvie?'

He frowned. 'I don't care for your calling me Mr. Darvie,' he said. 'Don't you think you could break down and call me Andrew? Just for one evening at least? I daren't suggest more in case I upset such a stickler for hospital etiquette as yourself. I'm afraid you'll not approve of all this modern freedom of expression?'

I smiled. 'Of course I'll call you Andrew,' I said.

‘But am I really as bad as that?’

‘Worse.’ His eyes were mocking. ‘I’ll bet you even think of us all as Dr. So-and-So or Mr. Whatsit?’

‘Well, that’s true,’ I said unthinkingly. ‘It takes me ages to get used to things. I had been engaged six months when I still found myself calling Bill Dr. –’

My voice stopped suddenly as I realised what I was saying.

‘Dr.?’ he asked gently.

I looked at him. So he, too, did not know. His gaze had dropped to my hands.

‘I was engaged to Bill Blake once,’ I said.

‘Bill Blake?’ He frowned. ‘The Senior Medical Registrar?’ If he had not heard about me, I could see he had heard about Sheila Mandin.

‘Yes.’ I said the words for him. ‘The one who’s now unofficially engaged to the Staff Nurse in Margaret.’

He nodded. ‘Please forgive me, it’s not merely idle curiosity, it’s something I want to know.’ His voice was very quiet. ‘Has Blake been engaged to Nurse Mandin long?’

‘Getting on for three weeks now.’ And then I answered the unspoken question in his eyes. ‘He and I were engaged for two years. Never –’ I forced myself to speak lightly – ‘never have a long engagement, Andrew.’

His jaw set, but all he said was, ‘Whatever you say, Clare. If you’re ready, maybe we ought to push off to the Rugger revelries.’

The Medical School Ballroom was full. The small, senior lecture-room was now the improvised ladies’ cloakroom. I went in, and left my coat with Annie, the comfortable housekeeper of one of the students’ hostels, who was resplendent in black satin and long jet earrings.

'Hullo, Nurse Maitland! Nice to see you getting about again, duck. How've you been?'

I smiled as I handed her my coat. I was fond of Annie. 'I've been around, Annie. I had a holiday – and then we've been busy. You know how it is.'

'That's right, duck,' she said kindly. 'And what I always tells Nares is that you've just got to keep on and it'll all come out in the wash.' Annie was Mrs. Nares. Annie's advice was much the same as Matron's had been, with slightly different wording. 'There's a good light in that specimen cupboard, Nurse! And they've got a good mirror in there. You use it.'

'Is that allowed, Annie? I thought they always kept the microscopes locked on these occasions?'

'So they do, dear.' Annie smoothed her tight shiny skirt. 'But there, seeing as they forgot this time – and I know you won't do any harm – you nip in. See yourself lovely in there you can, Nurse.'

I did as she said, turned up the lights, and saw how right Annie was. I tidied my hair, re-did my face, dispassionately. I did not recognise either my face or my dress. Bill had said that colour was made for me. 'Bill had been right about one thing at least,' I thought dryly.

I heard some other girls come into the cloakroom and greet Annie. I pushed open the half-shut cupboard door, so that they too, might share my good light, then turned and replaced my compact and lipstick in my evening-bag. As I did this I heard one of them say, 'Who's Andy Darvie brought? I saw him hanging about outside just now. Did you?'

The other girl laughed, and at her laugh my heart sank.

'My dear,' said Sheila Mandin, 'haven't you heard? Clare – Bill's ex! The poor girl is quite desperate these days now Bill's escaped her clutches.

She's simply thrown herself at the only man in the hospital who hasn't heard what a wet blanket she is!'

The other girl said quietly, 'I don't think you are right there, Sheila. I can't see Clare Maitland throwing herself at anyone. She's far too shy.'

Sheila laughed again. 'Maybe you're right, my dear. Maybe. I only know what Bill's told me about her. Poor Bill, he had a dreadful time. She just refused to understand how he felt about me and wouldn't break the engagement off. He finally had to put it in writing. It was the only way he could make her understand. You know, I often think shyness is an excuse to hide a thick skin.'

They must have gone out. There was silence. I sat down on the broad shelf that ran round the cupboard. I had to sit. My legs had given way.

The door opened properly. Annie stood in the doorway, a massive, sympathetic form. 'There now,' she said, 'you don't want to take any notice of that –' She stopped, then started again, 'That Nurse Mandin!'

I stood up. 'It's all right, Annie. My own fault for eavesdropping.'

'It was getting to be a habit these days,' I thought bitterly.

'That's as maybe,' said Annie, 'but if we all have to pay for our faults, duck, then Heaven help us is what I says to Nares. Now, you run along to your young gentleman, and don't let what people say spoil your party.'

Andrew had his back to me. He was talking to a very tall, dark-haired man in tails. A man who seemed as surprised by my changed appearance as I had been myself a few seconds earlier. Our eyes met and I saw him stop talking suddenly. Andrew turned round to see why it was that Hugh Sanders was staring over his head.

'Why, hullo,' said Andrew. 'At last!'

'I'm sorry I was so long, Andrew,' I said, 'but I met an old friend in there, Annie Nares, and we got talking.'

Hugh said, 'Good evening, Nurse Maitland.' That strange, almost vulnerable expression had gone from his face. He looked as withdrawn, as remote, as was his normal appearance. Now he was looking over my shoulder. 'I haven't seen Bill yet,' he said conversationally. 'Where is he?'

Andrew glanced sharply from Hugh to myself.

'Oh,' he said quickly, 'he's around somewhere.' Which, of course, was quite true. Then he smiled at me, a kind, reassuring smile. 'And who is this Annie? And why does she live in the ladies' cloakroom?'

'Annie –' Hugh and I spoke together, then we both stopped.

'I am agog,' said Andrew. 'Who? Or whom?'

'She's a hospital institution,' I explained. 'She runs one of the student hostels, and she's married to Nares, the X-ray porter. She used to be a theatrical dresser and she regales our titivating with little stories of her days in The Acting Profession.'

Hugh said, 'Annie's been queen bee at the dances for as long as I've been at Augustine's. She was in the hostel when Bill and I shared a room there twelve years ago. She was a great friend of ours in those days. Saved our lives with pampering hot-water-bottles and our pockets with illicit cups of sweet cocoa. Give her my regards when you see her again, Nurse Maitland. I haven't had a word with her for years. I'd like to see her again.'

'I'll tell her, Mr. Sanders,' I said.

'Call him Hugh,' said Andrew cheerfully. 'This is

our Big Night Out. Go on, Clare – be buddies! Even with the First Assistant to the Cranial Unit, and a Master of Surgery to boot! You're both off-duty.'

Hugh Sanders frowned, fleetingly. 'Please do,' he said coldly.

Andrew raised an eyebrow. The change in Hugh's voice was obvious. I was about to make any sort of answer and pass it over, when Sheila Mandin with Jill Astey, the girl who had been with her in the cloakroom, moved past us on their way out of the ballroom. Sheila glanced my way, amused, patronising. I felt my back stiffen, and then I felt suddenly reckless.

I beamed at Hugh Sanders and said, 'I should love to!'

He started slightly and then he smiled. It was a funny smile, as if he could not help himself.

'Good.'

'That's settled,' said Andrew firmly. 'And I want to dance. Come on, Clare – or, rather, may I?'

'You may.' I slid into his open arms and nodded at Hugh Sanders.

'You're out of luck, Darvie,' said Hugh. 'You've struck a Paul Jones. I think I'll join in.'

'Let's dance this one out,' murmured Andrew into my hair.

'Whatever you say, Andrew,' I said gaily, and I saw Andrew was looking at me almost as oddly as Hugh had just done.

'Let them look.' I thought I was hollow with misery and humiliation inside, but I wasn't going to show it any longer. I was going to be the life and soul of this dance tonight if it was the last thing I did. So I was a wet-blanket, was I? Amongst other things? I hung on to men, did I? Clutched them?

Well, it was not going to be me who did the hanging on tonight! I was going to show the hospital that I had got over Bill Blake.

'Hey! Clare!' Someone gave my hand a tug and I found Angela was beside me, as we began to go round in a circle. 'Where have you been? What's happened? You look blooming. Or is it the dress?'

Angie had known me most of my life, but not even she had ever seen me in a raging temper. There was no time to explain even had I wanted to, so I said, 'I expect it's the dress!' and slid off into the arms of Mike Gill.

'This is good, Clare,' he said. 'I'm glad you managed to get off for this party. Does one a power of good, getting around!'

'Oh, I'm always around, Mike,' I said cheerfully. 'Only maybe you can't keep your eyes on more than one Staff Nurse at a time!'

It was a long Paul Jones and I seemed to dance with half the resident staff. I certainly danced with all those I knew well. Everyone but Bill. There was no sign of Bill yet, and my mind flashed back to that child in Margaret. If only Bill would come!

The music stopped again. Hugh was in front of me.

'Mine?' he asked.

It was peaceful dancing with him. It meant that for a few minutes I could relax. Leaving aside Andrew, who was new to Augustine's, Hugh was probably the one man on the staff who obviously did not know Bill and I had broken up, and who would not be interested if he had known. Hugh Sanders had little time for the lighter side of life. I thought what a relief it was to find one man who was concerned only with his work and his patients. When you work in the Theatre, you hear all the gossip of the hospital. Jenny was a great chatterbox. But not even Jenny had been able to raise any gossip about Hugh Sanders. We knew nothing of him, beyond the fact that he was an excellent surgeon and reputed to be the biggest glutton for work in the whole medical staff. I was thinking this as we glided round in a waltz.

He said, ‘You apparently enjoy these affairs?’

‘Yes,’ I said lightly. ‘They’re fun. Don’t you?’

‘Up to a point.’ Then he said, ‘I find it slightly surprising.’

‘What? The dance? It’s going on as usual, surely?’

‘Not the dance.’ He was silent a moment, then he added, ‘You.’

‘Me?’ I looked up quickly. Now I was the one to be surprised – by the hardness in his eyes.

‘Yes. I had no idea that all this was going on behind your mask,’ he said. ‘This –’ he shrugged slightly – ‘this blithe spirit,’ he said very dryly.

‘My mask?’ I did not understand him. ‘Do you mean my Theatre mask?’

‘Amongst other things,’ was all he said.

It was the last dance of the Paul Jones, longer than the others had been. A little while later he said, ‘I see Bill is not here yet.’

‘No. I don’t think he is.’

He tilted his head and looked down at my face, steadily. ‘Work?’

‘Yes.’ I nodded. ‘There’s a child in Margaret he’s worried about.’

‘I heard about her,’ he said soberly. Then, ‘But you, you have no worries?’

‘No. Should I have?’ Then I hesitated. Perhaps I should tell him. But somehow I lacked the courage. He would think I was asking for pity.

‘Well,’ he said as the music faded, ‘I never grasped that fidelity was exclusively a masculine virtue. But you and I may have different ideas on these things.’

The music stopped, the Paul Jones was over. Andrew was racing over the floor to reclaim me, and I did not know whether to laugh or cry. Hugh Sanders bowed, 'Thank you.'

Andrew took my hand and drew it through his arm. 'Would you care for a lemonade or cider? Or shall we sit down?'

'Let's sit,' I said. 'I see a space on that couch over there. If we don't take it now, there won't be a hope later. There's never any sitting room after ten at these affairs as a rule.'

Hugh said casually, 'Enjoy yourself, Darvie,' and began to move away.

Andrew was only a little taller than myself. His square shoulders were close to mine, and I felt the strength in the arm under my hand. That solid strength gave me courage.

'Oh, Hugh, just one moment.'

'Yes, Nurse Maitland?'

I pretended that I had not noticed that snub. That I thought it a slip of the tongue, and not intentional, as I knew it to be. I said, 'As Bill probably won't be able to get here because of his case, I was wondering –'

'Yes?'

Andrew half turned his head to look at me, then dropped his gaze to the dance-floor, which appeared to fascinate him.

'Well,' I said smoothly, 'I saw Sheila Mandin a few minutes ago. I expect she's alone, as Bill can't make it. As you're a friend of Bill's, I thought perhaps you might like to meet her?'

For the first time since I had known him, Hugh Sanders was at a loss. 'Sheila Mandin?' He frowned. 'Why? What has she to do with Bill?'

'You don't know about Nurse Mandin and Blake?'

asked Andrew lightly.

'Nurse Mandin? The Staff Nurse in Margaret Ward?'

'Yes,' said Andrew. 'That pretty fair girl over there. Surely you knew she and Bill have a –' he raised his eyebrows – 'an understanding, shall we say?'

Hugh was staring at me. 'She has? With Bill Blake?'

'It's almost official,' I said, copying Andrew's tone. 'Really Mr. Sanders, you should keep up with the inter-hospital relationships.'

'You should,' agreed Andrew pleasantly, 'or there's no limit to the mistakes you can make in a place this size, if you go around without confirming your facts.'

'So it would appear,' said Hugh quietly. 'Thank you for putting me straight. Of course I know Nurse Mandin.'

The music started again then. 'Well, now's your chance to renew an old friendship,' said Andrew. He smiled at me. 'Do you mind if we risk our chances of a seat, Clare? I'd very much like to dance with you again.'

'Of course I don't mind.' I smiled back gratefully. When I looked round, Hugh had gone.

'You know, Clare, I thought this party might be fun,' Andrew said softly as we danced. 'I didn't know how much fun. I'm so glad you came with me.'

'Oh dear,' I thought, 'things are getting out of hand.' Then I told myself not to be a fool. Just because I had taken Bill seriously, had believed what he had said, did not mean that everyone else was so simple. Andrew, as he himself would say, had been around. He would understand.

It was near the end of that endless evening when I discovered how much Andrew did understand.

'You've done all right,' he said suddenly, 'more than all right, Clare. All the flags flying and none to know how much it hurts.'

'Andrew!' I gasped. 'How did you know?'

He did not answer my question; he asked another. 'How old are you?'

'Twenty-six.'

His eyes smiled into mine as we danced. 'I would have said you were younger. I expect it's that pristine quality you carry about with you. I'm three years older than you. The eldest and only bachelor in my family. My brother is married. Perhaps you know that?'

'No.' How could I possibly know? Until this moment I did not even know he had a brother.

His jaw set in a way I now recognised as a sign that he was upset about something.

'I doubt that it would have made any difference to you if you had known,' he said oddly, then he went on, 'Well, I'm single for the same reason that you are single. It's a silly reason, as old as the hills. But that doesn't stop it hurting.'

'You were engaged, too? Andrew, I am sorry.'

He smiled wryly. 'It's not much fun, is it, Clare?'

I shook my head. 'Not much.'

We danced in silence for a few minutes, then he said, 'Perhaps I'm not strictly honest when I say mine broke up the way yours did. But we have some aspects in common. Like you, I thought everything in the garden was lovely, and then, one fine day, I found it was not! I should have had the sense to realise it never is. But when one's in love, sense is not a word one has much use for. You know,' he said gently, 'you're not the only mug in this or any other hospital. In fact, you're not a mug at all. You're just a sweet, gentle girl, who fell in love with the wrong chap.'

'You're awfully kind, Andrew,' I said. 'But I can't tell you how sorry I am. Has she – has she married someone else?'

His jaw set again. 'No,' he said surprisingly. 'As I said, it wasn't quite like this affair of yours. All that happened was that I discovered she wasn't in love with me – never had been.' His eyes were very hard. 'It was just a convenient arrangement for her.' Then he smiled. 'You wouldn't understand that, would you, Clare?'

I said, 'I don't know. I don't think so. But why did she break it off?'

'I broke it off,' he said abruptly. He saw the unspoken question in my eyes, and nodded. 'Yes, I still love her. But I broke it off.'

I said, 'I may not understand, but I think you have been very brave.'

He shook his head. 'Not brave. Practical. Also, although I'm afraid I may take life more lightly than yourself, when it comes to getting married, I'm good and old-fashioned. One marries for love, or one doesn't marry at all.'

'But one doesn't get married for any other reason.'

'You wouldn't,' he said. 'But not everyone feels quite so strongly about this as yourself.'

I wondered what he meant, and why any girl should behave to him as he had told me. I could not make any sense of this, so I asked, 'Was that why you changed hospitals?'

'Yes. And of course the fact that this is a first-rate job to get. I wanted to make a clean break, get to know a different set of people, start fresh where no one knew about –' he hesitated – 'her. I think I was right. I think this is the thing.'

I hated to press him, and yet I had to know. 'Does it ever stop hurting?'

'It either wears off, or you learn to live with it,' he said thoughtfully. 'I'm not sure which. Somewhere between the two. Until you meet someone else. That's the real antidote, impossible as it may seem to you now.'

'Have you?'

He looked over my shoulder. 'I can't answer that truthfully at the moment, Clare. Yesterday, I would have said no, but tonight, seeing you, so sweet, so different from *her*, I don't know.'

'You mustn't get the wrong idea about me, Andrew,' I said quickly. 'This is all a line. I couldn't keep this up for more than one evening. I got angry tonight, angrier than I can ever remember being, so I decided to play a part. Don't be taken in by my act.' I smiled. 'I'll probably turn into a pumpkin or a glass slipper at midnight, and you'll see me as I am.'

He laughed suddenly and his arm tightened round my waist. 'I'll hang on firmly, and prevent your slipping away!'

I suddenly felt someone's gaze on me. We were dancing at the edge of the floor, and as Andrew said those words we passed Hugh, who was standing against the wall, watching the dancing. He could not have helped overhearing Andrew's last sentence. But even if he had heard, I could not understand why he should be looking as annoyed as he did. What could it matter to him what Andrew said to me?

I looked back at him, because I was curious. He was still frowning, but he had stopped watching us and was looking across the floor. Then I realised his frown, almost certainly, had nothing to do with Andrew or myself. Hugh was staring at Bill, who had come in and was dancing with Sheila.

Andrew was dancing slowly. Bill and Sheila danced by a few seconds later, and as they did Bill gave me a brief smile. I leant back in Andrew's arms, 'Bill, how is the patient?'

‘My small girl?’ Bill smiled properly and my heart turned over. He jerked a thumb upwards. ‘The stuff is working, praise be. She should do.’

I said, ‘I’m so glad.’ I saw Sheila glance coldly at me. Andrew’s face was anxious. I did not mind. This was something apart from any of us, something I had to know. I knew Bill would understand. Sheila could think what she liked.

The next dance was a waltz. We had just started when someone tapped Andrew’s shoulder and Hugh’s voice said, ‘Do you mind if I cut in, Darvie?’

‘I do very much,’ said Andrew, letting me go. ‘But you’re bigger than I am, Sanders, so I’ll bow out gracefully. If you’ll excuse me, Clare?’

I smiled. I was very tired now. ‘Of course.’

Hugh drew me to the centre of the floor. ‘I’m sorry to break in, but I thought it might be a good idea if you and I had a little chat, Clare.’

‘Why?’ I knew quite well, but I was in no mood for Hugh Sanders’ sympathy.

He said slowly, ‘I seem to have been putting my foot in things fairly consistently since we first met three weeks ago.’

‘Have you?’ I said lightly. ‘I haven’t noticed.’

‘I’m afraid I must have upset you rather badly. I’m extremely sorry that I should have done so.’

He was so very much taller than Andrew that I had to tilt my head back to look at his face.

‘Forgive my saying it, Mr. Sanders, but don’t you think you are inclined to over-rate yourself? Why should anything you say upset me?’

He was very pale, and I wondered if, like myself, he went white instead of red when angry. All he said was, ‘Why, indeed?’ and we finished the dance in a strained silence.

# CHAPTER FOUR

Next day I thought over what Andrew Darvie had said about making a break. The more I thought, the more I liked the idea. I thought about the dance, too, and about Bill and Sheila.

I did not think at all of Hugh. I had had quite enough of Hugh Sanders for the moment and was only sorry that I would have to see him in the Theatre daily.

The reason I did not think of Hugh was because I knew I had been rude in refusing his apology. I hated the memory, and was irrationally annoyed with him for being the cause. And, after all, he should not have jumped to conclusions. Even had I been still engaged to Bill, what right had Hugh Sanders to lecture me as to how I should or should not behave?

'The trouble with that man,' I told my friend Angie, as we discussed the dance together in my room that evening, 'is that he is convinced he is as right about life as he is about which instrument to use in the Theatre! Which makes him quite insufferable!'

Angie laughed. 'I'm so happy to see you getting worked up over something again, if only the unfortunate

Mr. Sanders. It's a good sign. You were never a rowdy girl, Clare, but you've been sub-human lately. Too good to be true. And too much of a doormat.'

I said, 'I gathered that.' I told her how.

'You poor thing,' she said gently. 'How miserable for you, hearing all that.' Then she said, 'What are you going to do about things?'

'I don't know,' I said in desperation. 'Just go on.' I got out of my chair suddenly. 'No, I'm not. I'm going to have a talk with Matron.'

I spoke to Sister Theatre on Monday morning, before I had my interview with Matron. I both liked and respected Sister, and I wanted her advice. Also I did not want her to feel I was doing anything behind her back.

I said, 'Sister, would you mind if I broke my contract and left the Theatre?'

She said calmly, 'I should mind, very much indeed. But I wouldn't stand in your way, if that was what you really wanted. Is it?'

'I don't know,' I said truthfully, as I had said to Angie. 'I just feel I must have a change. I want to do something different for a while. But I'm not sure that I want to leave the hospital for good.'

'Well, you run along to Matron,' said Sister. 'She'll give you the best advice. And you can tell her that you have my blessing, and that I will look forward to your return.'

Matron was as sensible and as matter-of-fact as I had expected. 'What you really need is a good, long holiday, Nurse Maitland. Can you afford it?'

I said, 'I'm afraid not, Matron. A fortnight is as much as I can run to.' She nodded her understanding. 'In which case we will have to find you a quiet post. After all, a change is often as good as a rest.'

'I'd prefer that, Matron. I'm not very keen on having too much time on my hands.'

'I never consider time on one's hands to be a good thing, Nurse,' she said firmly. 'I'll have to think.'

'Yes, Matron. Thank you.'

She said, 'Have you ever done any private work?'

'No, Matron.'

'Have you ever been to Scotland?'

'No, Matron.'

She smiled. 'Then what I am about to suggest will certainly be a change. Sir Inister MacFallor was talking to me only yesterday about his mother. She suffers from chronic rheumatoid arthritis, and is bedridden. It appears that Miss Davidson, one of our old nurses, who has been looking after her for some years, is badly in need of a rest. Sir Inister was saying how much he would like to send Miss Davidson on some sea trip, but the difficulty lay in his finding a suitable substitute to take care of his mother.'

She let this sink in for a few minutes before she went on. 'I think you could take that post, Nurse Maitland. It might suit you very well. The fact that it is in a quiet and isolated part of the Highlands, which is one of the problems that is worrying Sir Inister, will not bother you at all. It will give you a rest, and you will be earning at the same time.' She folded her hands neatly on the desk in front of her and looked at me steadily. 'The hospital will certainly give you leave of absence for a few months, and then, should you decide to return, it will be quite convenient for you to come back to your present position in the Theatre.'

I murmured, 'Thank you very much, Matron.'

She said, 'Talk it over with Sister Theatre and your friend, Sister Elizabeth, and let me know the answer in a day or two, if you like.'

On an impulse I said, 'I would like to accept now, please, Matron.'

She smiled. 'Think it over, all the same, Nurse. But I will tell Sir Inister that I have spoken to you, and perhaps he will have something to say to you about it. That will be all, Nurse.'

My head was in a whirl when I left her office. I had expected Matron to suggest my resigning from the hospital, returning to midwifery, going to another hospital. This plan of my going to Scotland to nurse Sir Inister's mother was something I could not have imagined in my wildest dreams.

But it would be nice to have a patient again. A real patient, with a bed to be made, hair to be brushed, to be fed and cared for by me. A person to know and perhaps, later, to love. That was the only fault I had to find with the Theatre. We seldom saw our patients awake, and never had time to know them. It was interesting, often exciting work; we were always extremely busy in an orderly fashion, but it was not, at least to me, proper nursing.

Scotland in September. Yes, I would like it very much. Would it be cold yet? What sort of clothes should I take? And where exactly was Mrs. MacFallor's house? I had heard Sir Inister mention his old home so many times. Somewhere in the West. Loch Kreagh. That was it.

I was walking fast, my thoughts hundreds of miles away. I passed men in white coats and girls in white aprons and saw none of them.

Then one face lingered. A face that was always in my mind, a shadow in the shadows.

Bill said, 'You're in a hurry, Clare!'

'I'm on duty. I had to see Matron and now I have to rush back.'

‘I won’t keep you,’ he said. But he did not move. Weakly, I stayed still in front of him.

He said, ‘I was glad to see you the other night. And it was nice of you to ask after that child.’

‘I wanted to know about her. Angie Shane told me what had happened.’

He smiled. ‘You don’t change, do you, Clare? Solid as the rock of Gibraltar. If you don’t think it’s dreadful of me to say this after –’ he hesitated – ‘after everything, I can’t tell you how good it is to know that.’

I had already made up my mind about Scotland. Now I was doubly sure.

‘Always good old Clare in the Theatre?’ I asked dryly.

‘Don’t,’ he said quickly. ‘That’s not like you! No, what I meant was that it’s good to know there are people of your sort about.’ He flicked his stethoscope against his legs with a gesture I knew so well, and glanced at me sideways. ‘Steadfast is the word I want. No matter what happens, you still care.’ I must have looked startled because he went on, ‘I mean, you still care about the patients.’

I said, ‘I would be in another job if I didn’t. And so would you.’

‘I suppose that’s true,’ he answered thoughtfully. ‘Well, I won’t keep you. But it’s nice to feel we are still friends.’

‘Yes,’ I said flatly. ‘Isn’t it?’

Virginia Creeper is quiet, I thought as I walked on. So is ivy. Steadfast. Clinging. Clutching. Then, because even now I could not be angry with Bill for more than a few seconds at a time, I wondered why he had said what he had said.

I did not wonder long. Angie caught me up at that moment. ‘I’ve been hanging round reading the students’ lecture lists for the past five minutes! I’m longing to know what Matron said, and what Bill Blake was so serious about just now, if you care to tell me?'

'I may as well, Angie. Then perhaps you can tell me why he said it, because I don't know. Bill was anxious to tell me how good it was to know I was always there, a rock in the Theatre. Or words to that effect.'

Angie said, 'You are growing up, Clare. I've never heard you use that tone about that young man before.'

I shrugged. 'I'll tell you something else. Matron's offered me a job.' I told her about it quickly. 'If Sir Inister agrees, I'll take it.'

'Even after Bill's little speech just now?'

'What difference does that make?' I said wearily. 'All the more reason.'

'I wouldn't be so sure,' she said. 'But I'm relieved to hear you say it. Take a look over my shoulder, Clare, down the corridor.'

I was taller than Angie. I glanced round, and saw what she meant me to see. Outside the Dean's office, Sheila Mandin in mufti was talking vivaciously to Hugh. He was not speaking at that moment. He was leaning against the wall, listening to her and smiling down at her silver-gold head.

We had reached the Theatre entrance by now.

'Bill Blake is finding his unofficial engagement to the fair Sheila a very different cup of tea from his official engagement to you,' said Angie. 'You're a one-man girl, Clare. A pity in a way, but you are what you are. Sheila will do Bill a power of good.'

'But he can't be worrying about Hugh Sanders. He's one of Bill's oldest friends.'

Angie said coolly, 'And do you think a little thing like that would worry Sheila?'

'It mightn't worry Sheila, but you don't know that man Sanders! Why –' I told her how Hugh had lectured me over Bill.

She laughed not unkindly. 'It looks as if Sheila's going round administering poetic justice.'

'You're not serious?'

She said, 'You probably did not notice him at that dance, but he spent most of the evening with her. I know you loathe the man and couldn't care less, but I think he's very attractive and rather nice. I also think it's an awful shame that a little wretch like Sheila should upset him, when all she's after is another scalp.'

'Upset him?' I was so fascinated that for the moment I forgot my own affairs. 'Angie, no one could upset Hugh Sanders. He's imperturbable!'

'Don't you believe it,' she said. 'Remember I have most of his cases in my ward. He can get good and worried under that calm exterior, which is one of the reasons that I like him so much. He really cares about the welfare of his patients. But don't underestimate that girl's face. It really is lovely.'

'I know,' I said, and her eyes softened as she went on: 'I don't wonder Bill Blake is worried. He knows – who better? – that we are all human. He must have seen the way Sheila hung on to Hugh at that dance, even after he got there. And now he can't help contrasting his quiet years with you with his hectic weeks with her.'

'You don't think Sheila wants to break it off?' It was an effort to keep that sudden wild hope out of my voice.

She said no. 'To be utterly callous, which I think she is, Bill is the best bet. He's got that job and house all lined up, and a nice little private income of his own thrown in. Money and young doctors seldom go hand-in-hand these days. No. Bill is definitely up on Hugh Sanders, from her point of view.'

'But, Angie, he's a Master of Surgery, and way

above Bill in his job!

'I know that and you know that. So does Sheila. But she's not interested. Bill's a good doctor, but he's not in Hugh's class. And Hugh's not the type of man to bother about making much money. He just wants to use his hands, and use them for nothing, if necessary. Sheila's no fool; she sees that. And when she's bored with him she'll rush off and become Mrs. Bill, unless some other unfortunate young man, with a larger private income, appears in the meanwhile.'

'I expect you are right,' I said hopelessly. 'Angie, I must go. Sister will be wondering where I've got to.'

'Well, you tell her you've decided to go to Scotland, and don't let anything that I, or anyone else has said, put you off. You get away, Clare, and see how things look from the outside. It's all too close to you here. You haven't had any chance to get things straight. Don't let this opportunity slip by.'

Sister Theatre said much the same when we talked it over that evening as we polished instruments together in the empty Theatre. 'I think you should go, Nurse.' She smiled. 'I don't want to lose you, but I think you ought to go!'

I laughed. Sister and I were good friends these days, and with me, when we were alone, she talked as to an equal.

She reached for the polish. 'Really, the way some young women behave at times staggers me!' She shook the tin fiercely. 'Still, perhaps we should be charitable. Matron can't really be blamed if our medical staff persist in making fools of themselves, but oh, how I wish they wouldn't do it!'

It is never any good getting surprised at the way news travels in a self-contained place like a hospital.

Everyone always knows everything that goes on. This may seem strange, when you consider how vital is the work done in a hospital, but that possibly is the reason. The grapevine of gossip is one of the relaxations we all enjoyed. We could not be petty in our work, so in our lighter moments our conversations became that.

'You're speaking in the plural, Sister?'

Sister said, 'Do you recall what I said about Mr. Sanders the day you got back from holiday?'

'Yes, Sister.'

She grimaced. 'I'm pretty certain now that I was right.' She rubbed the delicate forceps in her hand carefully. 'I don't care to discover that. I dislike feeling infallible. Certainly I have never been wrong about that one thing yet.'

'Which thing, Sister?'

'I've never failed to spot a surgeon in love before,' she said calmly, testing the grip of her forceps. 'Which is not to be surprised at, after all the years I have spent in the Theatre. But I'm sorry.'

I smiled. 'You don't approve of married surgeons?'

'On the contrary! I wish they all had to be married before they were let into the place. Think how much more peaceful life would be! But there, when you consider that we have a few hundred young men and young women working together in this establishment, you can hardly wonder if they fall in love. But how I wish they wouldn't!' She shook her head ruefully.

I had to laugh at her mock despair. 'Was it as bad in the old days, when nurses had to leave if they got engaged?'

'My dear, it was worse! The whole place intermarried. But to be serious for a minute, no, it wasn't. It was a much better arrangement, I consider. There was none of this shilly-shallying "shall I marry Jane or Mary or be just Good Friends" attitude, which I do abhor, and which causes so much trouble. Young people had to be sure of their minds, when an engagement meant the end of a nurse's career.' She sighed. 'I cannot count the happy marriages I know which started in this very Theatre, in the wards, and the lecture-rooms. But they were all straightforward. Nowadays!' She shook her head at the row of instruments on the trolley before her. 'Why these girls cannot be content with their own young men, I cannot understand. And it makes me very cross when I see one of my finest surgeons put out. Not in his work,' she added quickly, 'but in his mind.'

I said, 'Is he really serious about her, Sister? I thought it only started at the dance?'

Sister said primly, 'We have no business to be discussing personality this way.' Then her dimples appeared. 'But since we have started we may as well go on. Yes, I'm afraid I do consider he is serious. That is more a personal observation than anything else. Mr. Sanders is a serious man. I can't see him falling in love lightly. And as for it only starting at the dance – well, something has been wrong with him for the past three or four weeks. Sister Margaret tells me that the young woman in question is now quite open in her admiration for tall, dark surgeons And one must remember that the more clever a man is, the more foolishly he seems to fall in love.' She glanced at me. 'You are not going to let this affect your plans?'

'Would it be any use if I did, Sister? I can't compete with her.'

She said, 'Forgive me, Nurse, but are you still in love with Dr. Blake? If you are, I think you should go.'

I said 'Yes.'

She did not answer; she was looking over my shoulder. When she spoke next she had raised her voice. 'Can I do something for you, Mr. Sanders?' I turned to see Hugh standing in the doorway that led to the duty-room.

'I brought the list for tomorrow's cases, Sister,' he said.

'That's very good of you, Mr. Sanders.' She smiled up at him. 'I was just deploring to Nurse Maitland the fact that this hospital has become so – so democratic. Things have changed greatly in the past decade. When I was senior Staff Nurse in this Theatre I never saw one senior resident like yourself doing his house-surgeon's work. You mustn't spoil the young men!'

He came in and stood between the high stools on which Sister and I were perched. It was the quiet hour after eight, when all the junior nurses were at supper, the cases over for the day, the porters off-duty, the Theatre at peace. But the Theatre was set, as always, for an emergency. We needed only the twenty minutes necessary to get the steam going in the sterilisers to be ready to deal with any operation.

Hugh said lightly, 'You don't sound as if you approve of the change, Sister?'

'I'm old-fashioned, Mr. Sanders.' Her dimples deepened. 'But perhaps I do – in some ways. Only some.'

He smiled. 'When I was in the States, Sister, I used to wonder occasionally how you would have taken to life in the Theatre there.'

I picked up the artery forceps I had just put down. 'They call these things "snaps", Sister.'

'My good young people,' said Sister placidly, 'may I remind you we had a war a few years back? Many is the American surgeon I have had in this Theatre – and many is the time I have been called "Super-Charge" and “honey”!’

‘Which did you prefer, Sister?’ Hugh sounded amused.

‘Honey,’ she announced and we all laughed. Then she said, ‘Have you heard I’m losing my Staff Nurse, Mr. Sanders?’

‘Your Staff Nurse?’ he frowned slightly. ‘Nurse Evans leaving?’

‘I have two Staff Nurses,’ she said as the telephone bell rang.

I was on call. I jumped up. ‘My night,’ I said automatically.

Sister stood up at the same time. ‘Then you might as well sit down for a few more seconds. I’ll take it.’ She went into the duty-room and shut the door.

I looked at the trolley. ‘Do I go on – or do I put these away?’ I wondered aloud.

Hugh said, ‘Are you expecting anything?’

‘There is an appendix in Mary Ward. She came in this evening. But the poor girl has a nasty chest cough, and they don’t want to do it tonight if they can help it. I suppose they’ve found they have to.’

Sister put her head round the door at that moment. ‘No case. Outside call for me,’ she said, and shut the door again.

I climbed back on my stool again and took up the soft leather polishing-cloth. Hugh said, ‘Are you leaving?’

‘Yes.’ I glanced up at him. ‘It seems you were right and I was wrong, after all.’

He frowned again. ‘I don’t follow you, Nurse?’

I smiled faintly. ‘You were always anticipating my departure, Mr. Sanders. Correctly, as things have worked out. Only you had the wrong reason.’

‘I’m sorry. I really am sorry. I’m afraid –’ then he stopped.

‘Afraid of what, Mr. Sanders?’

He said quietly, 'Does it matter, Nurse? I realise that whatever I may say is unimportant.'

I looked at him properly now. There was something in his voice that I did not recognise. Then I saw his face, and I knew what it was. He was uncertain. 'They are right,' I thought. 'There is something wrong with him.' And then I thought, 'That's why he was so shaken at hearing about Bill and Sheila! She had kept him in the dark as Bill had kept me in the dark!' And I remembered how he had looked when he saw Bill dancing with Sheila.

I could not like him, but I could feel sorry for him. I was very sorry now that I had been so rude to him.

'Mr. Sanders,' I said suddenly, 'I feel rather badly about you.'

'About me?'

'Yes.' It was difficult to go on, with him looking at me that way, as if we were on different sides of a glass wall. But I could guess how he must be feeling, and I knew only too well how when you are really upset, any minor unpleasantness can hurt disproportionately. The fact that I did not like him did not make me want to hurt him.

'I'm sorry I was rude to you the other night at that dance. I shouldn't have said what I said, and I'm ashamed. Please forgive me.'

He was silent for a few seconds. When he spoke his voice was almost nervous. 'I deserved what you said.'

I said, 'Well, never mind. It's all over now.'

'Is it?' His long finger played with the line of instruments. 'Is it?'

I remembered Sister's last words before we saw him. He must have heard her question and my answer.

I said, 'Did you hear what I said just now?'

He made no attempt to prevaricate. 'I'm sorry. Yes.'

'Well, then,' I said bleakly, 'you must know it's all over. And it's time I moved on.'

He pushed his hands deep into the pockets of his long white coat. His hair was very black against the white painted walls and the smooth white ceiling. He straightened his shoulders, the way he always did at the end of a long case, when he was tired.

He said, 'I know just how you feel, Nurse Maitland,' and, as he spoke, his expression softened and was strangely kind.

Someone knocked on the double door. I called 'Come in,' and Andrew Darvie pushed one side open cautiously.

'All clear? Do I need a mask?'

'The light isn't on. We aren't working.'

He said, 'I saw the light was off, but I heard voices, so I thought I had better be on the safe side.'

I stood up. 'Have you come for your last injection?'

Hugh looked curious. 'What are you having, Darvie?'

'My boss is afraid my hand will drop off, so he's plugging me with penicillin,' said Andrew happily. 'Or, rather, Nurse Maitland is doing the plugging, which is far more pleasant! Didn't you hear how I harpooned myself last Friday?'

Hugh shook his head. 'I didn't. Bad luck. How is it?'

Andrew said, 'The trouble with you big men is that you really do walk around with your heads in the clouds. It's grand, thanks. It was only a minute scratch, but I am becoming the perfect malingerer! And it's a cast-iron excuse for coming to the Theatre out of hours.'

Hugh said colourlessly, 'It must be.'

At twenty-past two the next afternoon Andrew stood back to let Sir Inister precede him into the Theatre corridor.

'Thank you, my boy,' murmured Sir Inister absently.

The morning head-list was over, the afternoon of general surgery was beginning. Andrew was the first of the general surgeons to arrive. I went out to meet Sir Inister.

'Did you want Sister, Sir Inister? She's in the Theatre, but I'll call her at once.'

Sir Inister removed his spectacles and rubbed his eyes. He looked very old at that moment, far older than his real age. It had been a long morning for him.

'Would you like a cup of tea while you are waiting, Sir Inister?'

'I would enjoy a cup of tea, Nurse Maitland,' he said briskly. 'I always enjoy a cup of tea. But I did not come to see Sister. I came to see you. Now then, what's all this foolish nonsense I hear about your wanting to leave the Theatre?'

Over his shoulder I saw Andrew turn sharply, then he moved on into the Surgeons' room.

Sir Inister glared round the duty-room. 'Well, young woman! Where's this tea? And I don't care for it stewed! And no sugar!'

'It's here, Sir Inister.' I relaxed. I suddenly remembered how fierce Sir Inister always was in the Theatre when he was satisfied with a case; how charming when he was worried. The fact that he now seemed ready to bite off my head showed he must approve of Matron's suggestion.

He took the cup and saucer from me and frowned at the contents. 'Just right!' he said sharply, then without any change of tone he went on, 'I can't imagine what gets into you young women these days! You always have to be dashing off somewhere! But Miss Davidson's very tired, and since you have

Matron's recommendation and permission, I suppose we must consider it settled! Eh?'

I said uncertainly, 'If it's all right with you, Sir Inister?'

'And why should it not be all right with me?' he demanded. 'Am I such a curmudgeon?' Suddenly he smiled. 'Of course I am! But I never heard such nonsense in all my life! A first-class Theatre nurse wanting to go into semi-retirement looking after a frail old lady! But if that's what you want –?'

'It is,' I said fervently.

'Then we'll be pleased to have you.' He held out his cup. 'Another cup, please, Nurse Maitland.'

He tilted his head to one side and pursed his lips as he watched me pour out the tea. 'No sugar – oh, good girl, you've remembered! Thank you.'

I said, 'Thank you, Sir Inister. I'm so glad you think my taking Miss Davidson's place will be all right.' I hesitated, then I said, 'You don't think Mrs. MacFallor will object to the change?'

He fixed his pince-nez on his nose and stared at me. 'I always considered you a sensible girl, Nurse Maitland! Never thought you went about asking foolish questions! Why should my mother object? I'm her son, aren't I?'

Fearfully, I agreed that he was.

'Well, then, she knows I wouldn't send her anyone unsuitable. I shouldn't be a bit surprised,' he went on gloomily, 'if you and she didn't hit it off very well indeed. She likes young people, does my mother.'

I opened my mouth to thank him again, decided I did not dare and closed it without speaking.

Sir Inister glanced up at the duty-room clock. 'Can't waste any more time in here,' he said as he carefully replaced his cup on the tray.

'Got a cluster of students hanging around outside waiting for me to instil some knowledge into their thick young skulls. Better be off.' He held out his hand.

'I hope you'll be very happy in my home, my dear,' he said kindly. 'I know my mother will do her best to see you are. Thank you for helping us out.'

I gave him my hand. 'Thank you very much, Sir Inister. I'm sure I shall.'

Jenny, who had been hanging around the corridor waiting to change, rushed in the moment he had gone. 'What was the old man taking tea with you for, Clare? I never knew you and he were such buddies!'

'We aren't,' I said, then corrected myself. 'Perhaps we are.' I told her roughly what we had been discussing.

'Clare, what a marvellous idea! Is this official or a dead dark secret?'

I smiled. 'As official as you like. He'll tell Matron this afternoon, I expect, and I'll see her myself in the morning. But there's no point in keeping anything hush-hush – you know what the old man is!'

Jenny grinned. 'As big a chatterbox as I am myself!'

Nurse Martin and I were clearing the Theatre that evening when Andrew came back for his watch. It had now become routine for him to leave this by the surgeons' sinks.

'On the desk, Mr. Darvie,' said the student nurse. 'I've just put it in there for you.' She picked up two buckets piled high with mackintoshes waiting to be scrubbed. 'Shall I do these now, Nurse Maitland?'

Andrew said, 'Thanks, Nurse, you are an angel!' He made no move towards the duty-room and I saw he had come to talk. I was generally glad to see Andrew these days; he was a pleasant person to have around, but at that moment we were very busy and I was in no mood, nor had I the time, for chatting.

I half-turned from the enormous bowl-steriliser which I was stacking. 'Have you finished the laundry, Nurse?'

'Not yet.'

'Then you had better do that first. They like it down by six.'

'Yes, Nurse.' She put down the buckets and vanished into the duty-room for the laundry book. I heard her slight gasp. 'I was sure I put it there!'

'I picked it up on the way in, Nurse Martin,' called Andrew. 'It's quite safe. You're not seeing things.'

We heard her laugh, 'That's good. Thanks, Mr. Darvie. You must be a mind reader.' Then she moved on to the Surgeons' Room to collect the used gowns and masks in there.

Andrew said quietly, 'I wish I was a mind reader. A very useful thing to be.' Then he said more slowly, 'Do you think this is your solution, Clare?'

I held down the pile of stacked enamel-ware, decided it needed more water to be covered properly, turned on the tap, tested again, switched on the electricity and shut the shining silver lid of the steriliser before I answered. 'Well, isn't it?'

He smiled faintly. 'It might be a case of out of the frying-pan and into the fire. It works out that way, sometimes.'

I looked up at his face quickly; his bright blue eyes were thoughtful. 'I doubt that I'll find that, whatever else I do find in the next few months,' I said. 'I imagine life will be pretty quiet in that house in the Highlands. That's just how I want it. I'm not much good at dealing with life with a capital L as you find it in a place like this. I can do with a little of what Sir Inister called semi-retirement.'

He said softly, 'You poor darling. You've had a

raw deal. But do remember Uncle Andrew's advice. Uncle knows. Watch how you go now.'

I was touched by the kindness in his voice and manner. 'That's very nice of you, Andrew.'

Nurse Martin pushed open the swing-door. 'I'm awfully sorry, Nurse, but I've missed the laundry. Shall I run it down myself?'

'Oh dear.' I pulled out my watch. 'Ten past. Yes, would you? Talk to them nicely and see if you can get them to take it. Then come back as soon as you can. We must be straight by half-past.'

When she had gone again, Andrew said, 'I can take a hint. I'll go away or you'll ask Nurse Martin to run me down to the Mess on one of her trolleys.'

I smiled and pulled the covering from the table, then began scrubbing the white enamel top. 'I'm sorry to seem inhospitable,' I murmured, 'but time, tide and re-setting the Theatre for emergencies wait for no man.'

He moved towards the door, then stopped. 'I'm afraid you'll be very lonely up there, Clare.'

'I don't think so.' I scrubbed on. 'I'm used to working alone a good deal.'

'That wasn't precisely what I meant. I was talking about a rather different type of loneliness.' He smiled wryly. 'The nasty little brute one carries around inside oneself.'

I put down my brush for a second and straightened my back. 'Andrew, I'm so sorry. I was forgetting. It must be wretched for you.'

He swung his stethoscope off his neck and twisted it in his hands. He stared down at it, as if he did not recognise what it was. Then he said conversationally, 'It has been wretched, at times. And now I've an uncomfortable feeling that it's going to be still more wretched. I'm going to miss you, Clare.'

'I'll miss you, too,' I said politely.

He grinned. It's a pity we don't speak the same languages, you and I. We get along very well, on our different levels. Do you understand what I'm talking about?' He shot the last question at me.

I picked up my brush again and re-soaped it. 'No,' I said truthfully. 'Not a word. I haven't for the past five minutes.'

He roared with laughter. 'But it doesn't bother you?'

I had to smile back. 'Should it bother me? Tell me if it should and I'll react accordingly.'

'My good Clare' – he controlled his laughter – 'it shouldn't. Nothing *and* no one should bother you. You are far too nice. In fact, that's part of the trouble.'

I glanced at the clock. (Where was Nurse Martin?) 'What trouble?'

He stopped smiling. 'That, Nurse Maitland, is something I don't choose to explain.'

I had bent down and was cleaning the legs of the table. I stood up, momentarily. 'Andrew, what *is* all this about?'

I was surprised to see him colour faintly. He said, 'I'm burbling. You don't have to take me seriously. But I was just thinking that it might be quite fun if, once in a way, you did.'

The room was small and full of dark, heavy, old-fashioned furniture. The plain narrow bed with the thin brass rails had been pushed back against one corner of the wall. From that corner Mrs. MacFallor could see out of the two windows that overlooked the dark brown water of the loch.

Painted family portraits hung in a neat row round the walls. Four small boys, solemn and dignified in white blouses with lace jabots and lace at their wrists, and one little girl in faded filmy blue, and an enormous sash in a deeper shade, the exact colour of the wondering childish eyes.

'My daughter Lucy,' said Mrs. MacFallor, and she smiled gently. 'Lucy was always as she was in that picture. So happy. Such a comfort.'

I had only been in Loch Kreagh House twenty-four hours, but already I recognised those last three words as the favourite words of my new patient.

'Such a comfort,' Mrs. MacFallor had said of Miss Davidson who was now on her way to Majorca. 'Such a comfort,' she had said when Sir Inister had paid his brief visit of one night, after driving me the whole way from London. 'Such a comfort,' she had said, when I had finished washing her and given her her breakfast this morning and then inquired what I could do for her. 'Such a comfort, Sister dear, to have a young person in the house again. Only –' and her eyes, which were as blue as her daughter's had been, clouded anxiously – 'are you sure you won't be too dull here, alone with us old women?'

Ailsa, the housekeeper, Janet, the cook, and Gilly, the housemaid, had all been with Mrs. MacFallor since she had come to Loch Kreagh House as a bride sixty years ago. They, and myself, were now the only occupants of the house.

'But you'll mind, Sister, Gilly was a wee lassie of fifteen then, Ailsa had explained. 'She's still not young, mind you, but she's no more than seventy-five. Mistress MacFallor, Janet and myself are all turned eighty, although I'll doubt you would think it.'

'I wouldn't,' I had said honestly. 'You and Janet look twenty years less.' I had said nothing then of the frail, white old lady with the cruelly stiffened joints whom I had come to nurse. At first sight, I had thought Mrs. MacFallor looked older than anyone I have ever seen. Only at first sight. When Sir Inister took me in to introduce me to his mother she had been asleep. Later, when she woke and opened her eyes, I forgot her age, and as I grew to know her, I never again remembered that there was any difference in our ages. I have never seen more youthful, bright, intelligent, happy eyes in any person, ill or well, I have since met.

Mrs. MacFallor had long white plaits and a thin white face. She suffered constant discomfort and almost constant pain. She never complained; she never grumbled; she never even pitied herself. She never had the time. She was fascinated by life, the newspapers, the wireless, the maids – whom she called 'the girls' – the comings and goings of every soul in Loch Kreagh village from the 'Postie' to the latest-born bairn in one of the crofters' cottages.

Today, my first day alone, she was concentrating on me. On seeing that I was not lonely, that I had enough blankets on my bed, had eaten the kind of breakfast I liked, knew about the posts, and how to work the wireless in my bedroom.

'Are you sure your mattress is comfortable, Sister dear? Sister Davidson preferred a feather bed on top of her hard mattress, but if it worries you, or you think it old-fashioned and unhygienic, perhaps you would rather do without it?'

'It's perfect,' I said quickly and smiled. 'It's all perfect, Mrs. MacFallor, it really is. Thank you very, very much.' I looked across at the window. 'And I've never seen such scenery.'

She smiled back gaily. 'I love it, my dear. I always have. I can never look my fill, which is why I have no curtains in this room. I like to lie and watch the water, and the sunshine, and the clouds coming down on the hills.' She sighed, not unhappily. 'I am very fortunate,' she said sincerely. 'It is always such a comfort.'

I finished her bed which I was remaking. 'Is that comfortable?'

'My dear, of course!' She sounded almost surprised. 'You've taken so much trouble. Now, what are you going to do with the rest of your day?' And there we were, away from herself and back to me.

She saw my eyes glance at her portraits. 'My family,' she answered my unspoken question. 'Reading from the mantelpiece, Angus, Charlie, Archie and Inister.' Her voice softened. 'And that is my Lucy.'

'Does your daughter live near?' I asked. 'Is she able to visit you often?'

Her voice never changed and her luminous eyes never faltered as she replied, 'Lucy never grew up. She had an accident in the hills when she was ten. She was climbing with her brothers, Angus and Inister. She fell and fractured her skull.' The old lady closed her eyes for a moment, then opened them and smiled up at me. 'I know the correct terms. Inister is not my son for nothing!'

I said, 'I'm so very sorry, Mrs. MacFallor. I wish I had not asked.'

'My dear,' she said kindly, 'how could you have known? And this happened such a long time ago. Nearly forty-five years have passed since I last saw my Lucy. You grow used to things in half a century,' she milled softly. 'Even to pain.'

I nodded; I could not have spoken had I dared.

'But I have often thought,' she went on, 'that Lucy's death was not wasted.'

'Sir Inister?' I whispered.

'Yes.' She could not nod her head, but she closed

her eyes in assent.

'Inister was fourteen then. Until that time he had never talked of being anything special, and since he was our eldest boy, we naturally assumed that when he grew up he would carry on here with his father, running the estate, seeing to the forestry. But after Lucy died, Inister was determined to be a doctor. And once he was qualified, he turned that determination to specialising in what is now his great work. I have so often thought, with such joy, of the mothers my Lucy must have made happy. Through Inister.'

'That's true,' I said. 'Even in the short time I have worked with him in the Theatre, Mrs. MacFallor, I have seen him save so many.'

She said simply, 'It has been such a comfort to me. I wish his father had lived to see it, and the other boys.'

'They also?' I murmured.

Again she closed her eyes in assent and again she smiled.

'There was another war, my dear. Our war, that happened before you were born. Inister was in hospital then, but the other three were soldiers. It was a terrible war for soldiers. All my boys were killed in France before the end of 1915.' She was silent for a few moments. 'It was too much for their father.'

I looked up at the portrait of the good-looking man in his thirties which hung between the two windows. Her quiet voice said, 'My husband. The year we were married.'

'He had a very fine face,' I said thoughtfully. I was thinking what an outstanding pair they must have made. Neither age, nor pain could touch the perfect bone-structure of the old lady's face.

'He was a very fine man, my dear, and goodness is something that shows even in young faces.'

I turned back to look at her and thought, 'It can transform an old face.'

'Inister had all these pictures moved in here when I found I had to stay in bed. He insisted that I should have all my treasures about me, where I could see them. He's been a dear son to me, always so thoughtful, so kind. He has made me so happy. And now he has sent you to me, and we must try to make you happy, too.'

'Oh, but I am,' I said. I felt ashamed. I was ashamed at my preoccupation with my futile little problems, ashamed at my bouts of self-pity, in the face of this astounding, wonderful, real courage. There was nothing insincere, nothing false about Mrs. MacFallor. She had fought her battles with life, and she had won.

Then I thought suddenly, had she not fought at all? Had she not accepted everything, not with a passive resignation, but with a spirit that did most literally soar above pain?

As I came to know her better in the weeks that followed I never altered in my opinion of Mrs. MacFallor. She lay in her bed, stiff, painfully stiff, and she made her pain an old friend, not an enemy. She was unable to feed herself, unable even to hold a newspaper, but she only regretted her illness when it meant that I, or one of 'the girls', must be inconvenienced by some need, for which there was apparently never any hurry.

'Whenever it suits you, dear,' or 'When you have a free moment, Ailsa. Not now, later.'

'And the Mistress never changes,' said Gilly one morning as she brought me my early tea. 'She's aye been the same all the years I have been with her.

You'll mind, Sister, I was not always the housemaid. I was the parlourmaid in the old days, when the Master was alive and before we closed the two top floors. But we've no call to be opening them again now, and we've no call for a parlourmaid, with Mistress MacFallor in her bed all the day.' She sighed nostalgically and straightened her old, corseted back. 'I mind a few years back, Sister, when we had the company, I was aye in black all the day.'

I drank my tea; got out of bed quickly, slipped into my dressing-gown, tiptoed out of my room and opened Mrs. MacFallor's door softly. My room was next to hers, in case she should need anything during the night. I had discovered, in my first week, that she would never call me at night. So I had taken to looking in on her twice during the night and again at seven, when Gilly called me, in case she wanted anything or was uncomfortable.

Last night had been one of her bad nights. I had made tea at a quarter to four this morning, and we had drunk it together, conspiratorially, whispering, like schoolchildren enjoying a midnight feast. It had been after six before she had settled again, and now, as I had expected, she was sleeping peacefully. She would probably sleep until the middle of the morning.

Despite my wakeful night, I was not tired myself. I seldom was these days. The wonderful air, the quiet, regulated life, the peaceful yet stimulating companionship which I received from Mrs. MacFallor all acted as a tonic to my whole being. I could think of Bill quite calmly now. The thought might hurt, but I could think. I no longer had to shut my mind to every stray thought, my ears to a chance tune on the wireless to which we had danced, or my eyes to the calendar which showed just how many more days were left for him at Augustine's, and then the day upon which he had planned to move down to his practice in Kent and his new life, without me.

I could even accept that Sheila would be going with him as his wife.

They were officially engaged now, and I expected them to be married shortly. There was nothing to stop them, and since Bill was changing so little – house, job, all were to be as he and I had planned them – might he not keep to the original wedding date (that had been ours) in late October?

Mrs. MacFallor was teaching me to accept facts.

I washed and dressed slowly, turning it over in my mind, and then quite suddenly I thought about Hugh Sanders.

I had heard of him from Jenny yesterday. She wrote regularly and gave me all the Theatre, and most of the hospital, gossip.

'*Jane Innes is doing quite well in your place, although Sister is being a bit sticky, the way she always is with new Staff Nurses. Funny how she reserves all her patience for new pros. But then they need it, poor little creatures! Sir Inister, in contrast, is exuding charm to Jane, which I regard as highly ominous! The poor girl doesn't know him as we do and thinks she's made a terrific hit. But even she can see she hasn't made a hit with Hugh Sanders! The sparks fairly fly when he does a case alone, and sometimes even when he's helping the old man. Myself, I don't know what's got into that young man lately, but really he's quite impossible. Icily cutting or icily polite, and I don't know which is worse. Either way I feel two inches tall.*'

I had smiled as I read that bit. Hugh Sanders had

had that effect on me several times.

'*He's due for a holiday soon,*' Jenny's letter went on, '*which I think A Very Good Thing. And talking of very good things, Mike and I are officially engaged. Isn't that splendid? It's a lovely ring. I asked Mike if Hugh had been crossed in love? But all Mike would say was no one ever knows what's up with old Hugh as he's not the chatty type and certainly the last man to wear his heart on his sleeve! When I asked what about Hugh and Sheila Mandin at the Rugger dance, the only answer I got was that a man had to dance with someone, hadn't he? And I had to be content with that! Really, you are well out of it! Only, being the busybody I am, I would like to know exactly what is wrong with Hugh Sanders these days!*'

I might be six hundred miles away from the hospital, but I felt I knew more than Jenny about the subject. Angie had written by the same post: '*I hesitated about this letter, Clare dear, and then thought that perhaps you would prefer me to warn you that the announcement is due in the papers any minute now. Sheila has informed the whole hospital that she is leaving at the end of next month, although I don't think she's told Matron yet. I gather Bill Blake leaves at the end of this month.*'

For all my new-found confidence, I had to put down Angie's letter there. It was some ten minutes before I read on:

'*But if it's any slight consolation to you, honey, which I know it won't be, since you aren't the type to be consoled by someone else's unhappiness, your pet aversion, Mr. Sanders, is wandering round the hospital, looking more forbidding and unapproachable than ever. At a rough guess he looks as if he doesn't know what's hit him. Who would have thought that wretched little blonde could affect these men like that? But there, the older I get, the more I say, "I don't understand them"! Not one little bit. All the same, I am very sorry about it. As you know, I do like that young man. I think he's a good man in every sense of the word. But I have to hand it to our Sheila. She's made a changed person of him.*'

Now, as I combed my hair, I thought idly how strange it was that both their letters should be filled by news of a stranger. Then I thought, it wasn't really so odd. Hugh Sanders was a strong and unusual personality.

I wondered casually about Andrew Darvie. I had had a couple of letters from him during my first week in Scotland. They were cheerful, chatty letters, very like Andrew himself. Andrew was another – and a real – stranger, but neither of the girls had mentioned him. I decided that this was because, although from another hospital, Andrew fitted so well in to Augustine's. There was nothing in the least remote or intriguing about a charming, light-hearted person like Andrew Darvie.

Andrew had not answered my last letter. I realised now that it was three weeks since I had written it. I wondered if I had offended him. Hardly. There had been nothing in my letter beyond how I loved this part of Scotland and how happy I was in the MacFallor household. And Andrew did not seem a man who would take offence easily. He was probably too busy, which I knew was a pretty fair assumption to make of any of the Augustinian surgeons.

# CHAPTER FIVE

Mrs. MacFallor was still asleep, so I went down to breakfast. I found Ailsa seated at the table, presiding over the teapot.

'The Mistress had a bad night, Sister?' she inquired anxiously after we had exchanged 'good mornings'.

'She did, I'm afraid.' I sat down. 'But I think she'll make up for it this morning.'

'Aye,' said Ailsa quietly, pouring my tea. She peered at me through her thick glasses. 'You are looking a wee bit pale yourself this morning, Sister. I am thinking you are needing fresh air.'

'I'll go for a walk after I have washed Mrs. MacFallor,' I promised.

Ailsa shook her head. 'You have been pale since yesterday, Sister. I am thinking you are not sleeping as you should. Do you get off again after waking up to see to the Mistress?'

I smiled. 'I slept very well, thank you, Ailsa.'

Ailsa apparently had something on her mind and was not to be put off. She shook her head again. 'The Mistress will not be happy to have you tired. Six weeks you have been here and not a proper day off. You should go out this morning for the day!'

'Not the day, Ailsa,' I said lightly. 'I couldn't possibly.'

'Well, the morning then, Miss Maitland,' said Ailsa firmly, and I knew she was serious. Ailsa only called me Miss Maitland when she had a point to make.

'Janet and I have been talking,' she went on, 'and we will see to the Mistress for this morning, at least. We can do it, you know,' she added quickly.

I said at once, 'I know you can, Ailsa.'

She sat back in her chair triumphant. 'Well then, off you go, Sister! This is a good day with Mistress MacFallor sleeping late.'

The early morning had been clear; the sky had been golden. Now the hills were topped by great black and grey clouds that scurried and rolled as I skirted the loch and began to climb the first hill. The path ran beside the burn, and sometimes the burn itself became the pathway.

I splashed through the shallow water and then walked on and up through the long brown-green grass. My boots were high and waterproof and I was dressed for rain. I climbed steadily for half an hour, and then I turned to look back. I sat down to take in that superb view.

The loch lay like clear brown glass at my feet and the house by the waterside from which I had come stood calm and unchangeable, its granite walls glowing pink in the morning light. The hills around were golden-purple with the dying bracken and the flowering heather.

I looked slowly all around me. Wherever I looked, I was alone. I felt at that moment alone in the world, alone with myself. When you have lived years in a community and, before that, in a busy doctor's household, with parents, brothers, patients and friends coming and going, unless you seek solitude it is something that never comes to you. I had never sought it before, because I had never felt the need. Living in a crowd had become a habit. Until these past weeks, I had not realised what a blessing and a balm it can be, to be quite alone. I had discovered that, as far as I was concerned, it was the only way in which to get to know myself.

I sat there, in that same spot, for most of the morning. And as I sat thinking, a good many things fell into place. One of those things was my realisation of the fact that you cannot live any part indefinitely. And with Bill always I had been acting a part. I had tried to be what I felt he wanted me to be, and that was not myself. I would never be a party-girl. I loved, and would always love, quiet things and people. Perhaps Bill was wise? Perhaps he had seen this, and realised that our marriage would probably fail because we were so different.

Had Bill been so unkind, after all? I knew he would enjoy life with Sheila. He was the same type himself. He might call me 'steady as a rock', as he had, at our last meeting, but did he really want that in his wife? If he did, he would never have broken our engagement. No. Bill wanted someone more exciting.

I smiled down at the old house suddenly. Dear Mrs. MacFallor, how much she had taught me in these few weeks.

The sun appeared, pale yet brilliant, between the rushing clouds over my head. I took out my watch and saw it was nearly one. I stood up almost regretfully and began to go down slowly through the long grass and the splashing burn to the road that ran by the loch.

Ailsa threw open the front door. 'That's better, Sister! You've a wee bit of colour in your cheeks now. London must be a cruel place!'

Gilly, who was standing behind her, echoed, 'Aye, cruel.'

'Don't blame London, please!' I said. 'I was born this way. Pale but interesting.'

They smiled and as they did I noticed something odd about Gilly. She had changed from her usual pink-striped cotton dress and was arrayed in a neat black, Edwardian parlour-maid's uniform.

'Aye,' she said again, answering the surprise in my face. 'We've company and the Mistress says you are to go up to her at once.'

'I'll shed my boots and go up,' I said obediently. 'Who is it? The Minister?'

Ailsa said no, and would I not be delaying, Sister dear. So I changed my boots for shoes quickly and ran upstairs to the first floor. Had Sir Inister decided to pay a surprise visit? But I realised at once that it could not be Sir Inister. There was no car outside. It must be a neighbour who lived within walking distance. An important neighbour, for Gilly to be dressed up. Gilly had worn her pink for the whole of my stay, and she greeted Mrs. MacFallor's friends as her own old friends, which indeed they were, after her sixty years with the 'family'.

'Come in, Sister dear,' called Mrs. MacFallor in answer to my knock. 'Did you have a nice walk? I was so pleased to hear you had gone out! And now I have a nice surprise for you. I have a visitor, a friend of yours, whom I am sure will be a friend of mine!'

A tall man had risen from his chair by the bed as I came into the room. He was standing with his back to the windows overlooking the loch. My eyes were not yet properly acclimatised to the light in the room after the clear air of the hills, but I recognised the outline of his head, even before he moved towards me, his hand outstretched and before Mrs. MacFallor went on:

'It is very kind of you to bring this letter from Inister yourself, and so nice that you should know Sister. We are so happy to have her with us, Mr. Sanders. She has been such a comfort.'

Hugh Sanders had come up to Scotland to fish. 'Sir Inister has advised me to spend a holiday this way for years,' he told Mrs. MacFallor. 'Somehow, there never was enough time to spare to get this far away from the hospital. But this year –' he hesitated – 'I decided to make time.'

'I think you have been very wise, Mr. Sanders,' she answered in her gentle voice. 'Don't you agree, my dear?'

'Indeed I do,' I said. 'I couldn't agree more. This place is perfect.'

I smiled down as she lay there, stiff as ever, her beautiful blue eyes so keen, so eternally youthful. 'I'm so grateful to you and Sir Inister for giving me the opportunity to be here with you.'

I saw Hugh glance quickly my way, as if he were surprised at something. 'My dear, you know how we love having you!' she said again. 'But I am afraid we have worked you too hard. Ailsa told me how concerned she was by your white face at breakfast this morning. I am so sorry you should have these disturbed nights.'

No one, listening to us, could guess that I was the nurse and she was the patient.

'Well, I'm not sorry, Mrs. MacFallor,' I said firmly. 'Apart, of course, from the fact that it means you yourself have not slept well. If I had not been awake this morning I would not have seen the sun rise over the loch. I wouldn't have missed that for anything.'

And to get off the subject of the night, I went on to tell them of my walk and the wonderful view from the hill.

'I've never seen anything like it,' I said. 'It was that one over there,' I nodded at the window. 'That hill on the left. I'm afraid it made me forget all about the time, which is why I am so late.'

'You are not late at all. But, my dear child, now you have started climbing, you will be careful?'

'Of course.' I was sure she was thinking of Lucy, her daughter. 'But you don't need to worry. I'm not really the mountaineering type. I just walk, then sit, then walk again.' I smiled. 'There's nothing intrepid about my hill-climbing.'

'I imagine Mrs. MacFallor is talking about the mist,' said Hugh.

I half turned to look at him. For a few moments I had forgotten he was there. I was quite surprised to find how easily he fitted into our set-up. It was, and this was odd, almost as if he belonged here, too. It was doubly odd, because I had never felt this about him in hospital, which was, after all, our normal environment. 'I wouldn't go out if there were a mist,' I said. 'I know I'm quite good at doing the wrong things, Mr. Sanders, but even I am not as foolish as all that!'

'My dear, you are not foolish at all,' remonstrated Mrs. MacFallor gently. 'And you never do the wrong thing.'

I laughed. 'Don't you believe it, Mrs. MacFallor! I can be as daft as a brush sometimes.'

She laughed, too. 'How delightful. I should love to see it!'

Hugh Sanders said, 'I think I must now agree with you there, Mrs. MacFallor. But I am afraid we are unlikely to be treated to the spectacle. I would hardly say that folly and Nurse Maitland have ever walked hand-in-hand.'

He held my gaze, as if he expected me to carry my point further, but I said nothing. I was thinking, 'I must seem as dull to him as to everyone else.'

Mrs MacFallor's eyes moved from his face to mine and then back to his again, reflectively. She said, 'Well, it all sounds most intriguing and you must talk to me more about this later, Sister. I see Mr. Sanders is your champion!'

I had seen nothing of the sort but I never wished to disagree with her so I merely smiled.

She went on, 'But we really must explain to you about the mists, dear. You've not been in the Highlands before, so of course you couldn't be expected to know about them, and since you've had so little opportunity for much walking in the time you have been here, I'm afraid I have forgotten to impress upon you how dangerous they can be. I must admit I was most unhappy this morning when Ailsa told me she had sent you out without a suitable warning.'

I saw she was serious and promised to be careful. 'I'll never do any climbing if there is any trace of one around.'

'There seldom is a trace when you start,' said Hugh soberly. 'They just come down on you quite suddenly, if you are high enough. And that doesn't have to be very high. You might well run into one round here. I should say it's all easy walking, which means you can walk into a cloud before you realise it.'

'The thing to remember, Sister dear, is that you must just stay perfectly still, wherever you may be,' said Mrs. MacFallor. 'Sit down and wait. Even at the risk of a chill. Better that,' she hesitated, 'than a fall. The mist will move after a while, it always does, and you will be able to go on again. If, by some misfortune you are caught in an unusually long one, you will always be found by someone who knows the hills.'

I repeated my promise to be very careful. 'And please, Mrs. MacFallor, don't be anxious. I really am not at all adventurous. My brothers plagued the life out of me because of my timidity as a child. I only fell out of the apple tree once a year, and then only because they had chased me up! I have no head for heights.'

Ailsa knocked at the door. 'Gilly is ready to serve the luncheon. Will I bring up Mistress MacFallor's tray now, Sister?'

'Thank you, Ailsa.' I glanced down at my clothes. 'Oh dear, I've only just realised I'm not in uniform. I'm so sorry.'

'Not at all,' said Mrs. MacFallor. 'How very nice! This is your day off, Sister, so why should you wear uniform?'

'Only the morning off,' I said quickly.

She said no, sweetly but firmly. 'Everything is arranged. Ailsa will give me my luncheon, and then, later, if perhaps you would settle me for my rest, I shall be most grateful. But only that. And now you and Mr. Sanders must go downstairs. You mustn't keep Gilly waiting. Don't forget Janet, either. She will be most upset if her food is spoiled.'

'Aye,' said Ailsa. 'Janet will, indeed.'

'It's very kind of you,' I said gratefully. 'Thank you.'

Hugh stood up. 'I had only meant this to be a morning call, Mrs. MacFallor. I did not mean to invite myself to a meal.'

She smiled up at him. 'What would Inister say if I let you leave his house this way?' Then her eyes clouded. 'Or are you expected elsewhere? We mustn't be selfish in our pleasure at your company. Have you friends waiting?'

He said at once, 'No, thank you. Only my hotel.'

Ailsa said, 'You are not thinking of getting back to the Loch Kreagh Hotel for lunch? On foot, Doctor?'

He smiled and shook his head. 'I have some sandwiches,' he explained. 'They gave me a packet before I left.'

'Dear me,' said Mrs. MacFallor. 'Sandwiches for a tall young man like yourself! Nothing like enough!'

Ailsa agreed, shocked. 'They will maybe come in handy for a wee snack before tea.'

Hugh opened the door for me and we went downstairs together, leaving the two old ladies to discuss in their soft voices the astonishing lack of appetite in the younger generation. I had been a constant source of amazement since my arrival because of my small capacity for food.

To fill the rather strained silence that had arisen between us now, I told Hugh about this. 'Ailsa can never get over the fact that I can't face porridge, two eggs and a mountain of baps for breakfast!'

He smiled as he held my chair for me. 'I must say that whatever they do feed you on seems to suit you. You look a different person, Clare.'

'I feel a different person. I would never have thought anyone could feel so different in five weeks.'

But he looked very tired, I thought. Even more tired than he had in hospital. His dark eyes were black holes in a paper mask; the skin of his face was stretched tightly over his cheekbones.

And he seemed older, and somehow no longer remote but sad. I thought of Angie's letter and how he must be feeling. That would explain a lot. 'Do you mind my calling you Clare?' he asked abruptly.

I said casually, ‘I thought we settled that long ago.’

He frowned slightly. ‘Long ago? At the Rugger dance, do you mean? By Andrew Darvie? I didn’t think we had taken it up.’

I said, ‘You made rather a point of not taking it up.’

He made no attempt to prevaricate. ‘Yes,’ he said quietly. ‘I did, didn’t I? I’m sorry. I hope you weren’t offended.’

‘Didn’t you mean me to be?’

He said, ‘You know, I had no idea you were quite such a forthright person. How do you want me to answer that?’

‘As you wish,’ I said lightly. ‘It really isn’t important.’

He half-smiled. ‘I’m glad that what I so stupidly said didn’t bother you. You don’t have to say it,’ he went on at once. ‘I’m not laying myself open to your rebuke again. I haven’t forgotten your telling me on that last occasion when we were alone together that I’m inclined to overrate myself. I’ve no doubt you are right.’

Gilly came in with the next course then, and I was never so glad to see her. When she had collected our plates and left again it was easy to start afresh.

‘Have you been up here long? When did your holiday start?’ I asked.

‘I arrived last evening. I drove up. My car’s at the hotel. I came over the hills this morning. They gave me the route and it wasn’t hard to follow. I must have passed quite near to where you walked.’

‘I didn’t see you,’ I said. ‘I’m surprised I didn’t. It’s so open up there.’

‘Not really surprising. You were probably thinking of the view and – other things. I would be the last person to cross your mind.’

That hadn’t been quite true of this morning but I was not going to say so. I said instead, ‘It is very good of you to devote your first day to Mrs. MacFallor.'

'Why?' he asked uncompromisingly.

I thought suddenly of Bill, who would never mix business and pleasure. '*A holiday is a holiday, Clare! On holiday I'm no doctor! Never even heard of a stethoscope. What is the thing?*'

'Well,' I said to Hugh Sanders, 'it's not a very exciting way in which to spend a precious first day. And you couldn't even have guessed what a perfect darling she is. I think it very nice of you,' I added slowly.

For the first time since I had known him he seemed actually embarrassed. 'I rather wanted to come. The Boss asked me, and –' he hesitated – 'well, so I did,' he ended almost lamely.

'I'm very glad you did.'

He watched me carefully. 'Are you?'

'Yes. You've given Mrs. MacFallor and "the girls" a great deal of pleasure. Gilly gets a terrific kick at the chance of dressing up in her best black.'

He smiled. 'You're happy here, aren't you?'

'I love it. I would never have thought I could love it so much, but I do. And it's so nice to be back, having a real patient again.'

He understood what I meant. 'I've often wondered what made you go into the Theatre at all, Clare. You aren't really the Theatre type. I would have said you were far more at home in the wards.'

'I suppose I am,' I said. 'But it just happened. You know how these things do happen in hospital?' He nodded. 'There was a vacancy for a Theatre Staff Nurse just at the time my set finished midwifery. I had enjoyed my Mums and Babies, but I did not want to go on as a midwife, and as I had won –' I corrected myself and added quickly, 'Matron offered me the job.'

I would not want to seem to boast to anyone but above

all to Hugh Sanders. My camouflage was not much good. He took me up at once. 'You had won what?'

'The Surgery Gold Medal.'

'Which made you a natural choice, on paper.'

'I suppose so. It was too good a job to turn down, and I liked Miss Oxenham, so I took it.' I drew a mental breath and plunged on. 'I had just got engaged to Bill then and my future seemed to lie outside the hospital, so I thought it would be an interesting experience, for a while.'

He did not answer directly; he did not even look at me. He stared out of the window to the loch and the hills beyond. At last he said, 'How do you feel about going back?'

'I haven't thought of it yet. I've another six weeks at least up here. But I think it will be all right, going back.' My voice fell of its own accord. I made an effort and added more brightly, 'And when I do, I think I'll probably ask Matron if there's a chance of my getting back to the wards eventually.'

'I'm sure you're wise,' he said calmly. 'You'll find they are all very glad to see you in the Theatre. Sister Theatre, I know, has missed you badly, and my Boss was saying only three days ago that he didn't know why he had sent that quiet young woman with the lovely eyes and neat hands on a wild-goose chase up North!'

I was too staggered to pretend. 'Lovely eyes, me?'

He smiled. 'I believe you are almost shocked. You needn't be, Clare. They are lovely.'

I had to smile back. 'You should hear my brothers on the subject. The colour of pure mud is their brotherly description.'

He said, 'Then I'm more glad than ever that I'm not your brother.'

I did not quite see the connection and I did not

want to pursue it, so I asked after Sir Inis' busy as ever? As tetchy as ever? And ho who had been riding pillion without That fractured skull he did on my last mo.

I was going to add the date, when Hugh said, 'She's done very well. She's going to get a with it. Another of the MacFallor miracles.'

We went on then into the safe realm of hospital 'shop', which we both knew and we both loved. It was the first occasion upon which we had ever really talked to each other at all, and I had a fresh surprise when I discovered how well Hugh could talk. He was serious and pleasant at the same time, with none of that lightness and undercurrent of flirtation that was always present with Bill and – now I came to think of it – Andrew Darvie.

In some ways, this man was so much more like myself, and we talked objectively. Yet while we did, he paid me a constant, unspoken compliment in his assumption that I knew what I was talking about and was worth discussing these things with. I had talked with enough doctors in my life to realise that although I might find it hard to like Hugh Sanders, from a doctor of his standing this was no small thing.

Bill had always told me of his cases but never, even when we had been engaged, had he asked my professional opinion on anything, or would have considered my opinion worth having if I had offered it.

But Hugh talked to me as an equal. 'Did you think she would do, Clare? Did you think we did right? And how about this chap? A boy I did last week.' And when he had finished explaining the details, 'What do you think?'

It was not just an idle, polite query. He meant what he said. He really wanted to know my answer.

Whatever my personal feelings about him, the nurse in me could and did appreciate that sideline of his character.

Mrs. MacFallor was very tired that night. 'My child, I do hope I do not disturb you again,' she said as I tucked her up.

I said, 'I enjoyed our clandestine cups of tea! And I have enjoyed my day.'

She smiled sleepily. 'Such an exciting day. And such a nice young man! And, my dear,' she whispered cosily, 'I do like a young man to be handsome.'

'How right you are, Mrs. MacFallor,' I teased gently, then thought a moment. 'I suppose he is handsome. I never really noticed it before.'

'Sister!' She was almost shocked. 'He's very handsome, and very charming.'

'He was today, I will admit.' Then I laughed. 'I mustn't be unfair to Mr. Sanders. I only know him professionally and usually when I see him, his face is hidden behind a mask.'

She murmured something.

'I'm sorry, Mrs. MacFallor, I did not catch what you said.'

She said, 'It was nothing, dear. Just an old woman thinking aloud. You mustn't take any notice. Now, you be off to bed. Is there a nice programme on the wireless for you to listen to?'

'There's a lovely concert. But first, are you sure you are comfortable? And is that head-shawl right?'

'Quite right, and so comfortable. Good night, dear. Please don't bother about me any more.'

I turned off the light and opened the door. 'Good night and sleep well. I'll be in at midnight. Take no notice of me unless you feel like it; but I'll be looking in.'

Half an hour later I switched off my own light and turned the wireless down low, to listen to the symphony in bed. As I did this, I realised that in that strange way that you sometimes do hear things after they had been said, I could remember what Mrs. MacFallor had murmured. She had said, '*And his feelings are also hidden behind a mask.*'

I smiled into the darkness. How much she saw, that old lady, and how wise she was.

I was fast asleep when I heard a soft knock on my door and Ailsa's voice. 'Could I come in, Sister? It's Ailsa.'

I sat up at once and turned on the light. It was seven minutes to two. 'Of course. Is Mrs. MacFallor wanting me?' I reached for my dressing-gown quickly. Mrs. MacFallor had been sleeping when I looked in at midnight.

Ailsa had come in quietly and closed the door carefully behind her. 'It's not the Mistress. She's fine. It is Angus Grant who is wanting you.'

'Angus Grant?' I rubbed my eyes. 'Has there been an accident?' Angus Grant was one of the ghillies at the Loch Kreagh Hotel. What could Angus want me for? Had something happened to one of the guests? In which case why hadn't they called Hugh? Or had something happened to him?

'Aye,' said Ailsa grimly. 'He is wanting you at once.

'Mr. Sanders?' My mind was on Hugh. I was out of bed now and fumbling for my slippers. 'I'll dress at once. What's happened?' I repeated.

'It is not Mr. Sanders,' said Ailsa. 'It is Angus's Jeanie. You'll know she is expecting?'

I was surprised at the surge of relief I felt that it was not Hugh. There was no time to work this out now, so I shelved the thought. 'Wait a minute,' I said. 'Yes. I do remember now. That pretty red-haired girl who came with that parcel from the Minister a while back? Mrs. MacFallor told me she was married to Angus. Next month the baby's due, isn't it?'

'Aye,' said Ailsa. 'That's what they told her at the clinic. But Angus is downstairs saying that he is thinking maybe the bairn will not be waiting another month and maybe Jeanie was mistaken about the time.'

'Tonight?'

Ailsa nodded. 'And the Doctor is over with Mistress Macintyre, the Minister's mother, at Kilkreagh, while the Nurse is away up the hills with Elspeth Ingles. It will be Elspeth's first, too. Mistress Macintyre is bad, the poor lady, so Angus was not wishing to get the Doctor back. It will be all of forty miles for him to travel in any case. Angus was minding to go to the hotel for Mr. Sanders, but Jeanie said she would like to have you as she is knowing you and perhaps after all it is not really time.'

'Well, we won't take any chances on that,' I said. 'So will you tell Angus I will be with him in a few minutes, and explain things to Mrs. MacFallor if she's still asleep when I leave?'

Ailsa's grim old face relaxed in a smile. 'Aye. I was sure you would be going. Angus will be very glad, the poor laddie. He is very worried.'

Mrs. MacFallor was awake when I looked in on my way down. I told her briefly what had happened. 'Ailsa will stay in my room until morning,' I said. 'I know she'll take good care of you.'

'Of course she will,' she said. 'But you tell Angus to take good care of you on those hills at this time of the night And give my love to Jeanie.'

'I will. Goodbye.'

Angus Grant, a short blond man in his early twenties, stood in the back hall, twisting his tweed cap in his hands.

'I am very grateful to you, Miss Maitland,' he said seriously.

I knew Angus fairly well, although I only knew Jeanie by sight. When he was not working up at the hotel, which lay seven miles away across the hills and fifteen by the narrow stone road, he was odd-job man to the MacFallor household.

'Don't look so worried, Angus,' I said, 'Jeanie's a fine girl.' To comfort him I used the old midwifery joke which never failed with first babies. 'I can truthfully say I have never lost a father yet!'

Janet, the cook, wrapped in grey shawls, was in the kitchen doorway. 'I have been telling him, Sister,' she said in her soft voice, 'you have brought many a bairn into this world.'

'That is so,' said Angus politely, but his face remained furrowed with anxiety.

'Thirty-seven,' I said honestly. 'Seventeen girls, twenty boys. Now, shall we go?'

The night air hit me in the face as he opened the back door. The air was heavy with damp. 'There will be a mist soon, I am thinking,' said Angus. 'Will you take my hand, Miss Maitland? It will be easier for you in this dark.'

I took his hand and we started on our way.

We walked round the loch, then up and over the hills, where the night was like a blanket of black, and the cold something that crept into your bones and stayed there We talked very little. The pace was faster than anything I had done alone.

I wished I felt as sanguine as I pretended to him.

But if Jeanie were right in her dates, and this baby was being born a month early, then anything – or nothing – might happen. Either way, I wanted to be there quickly.

At last I felt the ground under my feet straighten and then grow soft as we crossed the small boggy plateau of a hilltop. On that plateau was their cottage. In that cottage I found Jeanie and her condition was much as I had expected. What I had not expected, and was grateful to find, was electricity.

'Have you your box ready, Jeanie?' was all I asked. I had brought my own small surgical equipment with me but I had very few things and was relieved to hear her answer.

'Aye, I have that.' She explained that because of the loneliness of their cottage, the Nurse had left an emergency midwifery box, sealed and safe, with Jeanie weeks back, in case it should be needed. It was.

The dawn came slowly that morning. The clouds broke up and young sun came through as Angus and I sat down to breakfast in the one room that served for everything. Jeanie, in her bed by the wall, smiled, wearily happy, over her cup of sweet tea, her small daughter in her arms.

'Eighteen!' said Angus suddenly. 'Eighteenth. That's what the wee lassie will be.'

Jeanie looked as puzzled as I felt, and then I remembered. 'That's right, Angus. My eighteenth girl,' I told Jeanie. 'And the best!'

'Aye,' said Jeanie. 'Aye.' Then she said shyly, 'I would like to call her by your name, Sister.'

'Jeanie, how lovely! That's never happened to me before. My name is Clare. Is that all right?'

Angus inclined his head gravely. 'We would be

honoured to call her Clare, Miss Maitland. It is a beautiful name.'

We finished breakfast. I tucked up Jeanie, bathed my namesake-to-be and settled her in the old wooden cot that had been Jeanie's, and Jeanie's mother's before her. I lifted the cot and placed it by the bed.

'I'll tell you one thing, young woman,' I said as I stroked the small, round, petal-soft cheek with one finger. 'Your Mama can't count. I've no scales to bear me out, but if you are anything less than eight pounds, then I'm a Dutchman!'

Jeanie grinned cheerfully, 'Och, Sister, I have no head for figures!'

'Never mind,' I said. 'It's rather nice for you. You've saved yourself a month's waiting.'

Angus said soberly, 'It would not have been nice, I am thinking, if you had not been here, Miss Maitland.'

'Miss Davidson would have come,' I said.

Jeanie shook her head. 'Miss Davidson is not young. Crossing the hills at night is not easy for the old. And Miss Davidson has not done the Maternity, Sister.'

'I see.' I shut my mind to what I could see. It was all safely over now, but these little mistakes, that are not serious in a city, can make all the difference in an isolated country cottage. Jeanie was strong and sensible and would probably have been quite all right. But I would not like to take that risk myself, alone, in these hills.

'What about your work, Angus? And can you get Jeanie's mother?'

Angus told me it was all arranged, that Jeanie's mother would be up to help her daughter as soon as she heard the news.

‘I’ll be away to her before I go to the hotel. It’s no’ far, Miss Maitland. A wee walk to the other side of the loch.’

The ‘wee walk’ was eight and a half miles distance!

We agreed that I should wait until Jeanie’s mother arrived, and then make my own way back to the house. Angus was to telephone their doctor from the hotel, and then go to his usual work. He was booked for that day’s ghillying and could ill afford to lose the money, but he offered to cancel his work so that he might see me safely home.

‘Thank you, but there’s really no need, Angus. I can easily manage in daylight. I walked half-way here yesterday morning; the paths are very clear. Would you mind ringing the house for me, when you get to the hotel? Tell them about Jeanie – I know they’ll be anxious – and ask them to tell Mrs. MacFallor I’m on my way home?’ Angus promised to do this as he shook hands solemnly and gratefully.

When he had gone, Jeanie and the baby dropped off to sleep. I washed up quietly, tidied the room round them as best I could, and sat down to wait.

Mrs. Christie, a thin, beaming woman, who was a faded version of Jeanie, arrived a few minutes after nine. They pressed me to stay for another breakfast, but I was getting worried about Mrs. MacFallor.

‘I think I should get back. If you are sure you can manage, Mrs. Christie?’

Mrs. Christie’s grin nearly reached her ears. ‘I had eight of my own, Sister, and they all flourished!’

I grinned back. ‘Then I’ll leave you to it. And congratulations!’

The morning air was brisk and cold but there was no trace of the clammy chill of the night. The sun was clear of clouds as I started back over the burn-crossed plateau, but I saw that in the west the great white-grey monsters were sailing inland from the Atlantic. They did not worry me; I knew I should be home long before they reached me; for there was practically no wind on the hills this morning.

My foot stuck in a small bog once, then twice. The second time I nearly lost my boot. I sat down and heaved and eventually the mud-covered boot slid free. I went on again, more slowly this time, watching the ground carefully. I did not want to end up in my stockinged feet. The land descended and I was down the first hill, I had to climb again far higher this time, to go over the crest of the hill that now lay between myself and the loch. I hurried upwards, keeping my eyes on the path. I did not want to lose my way and I had discovered it was easier to go fast up rather than down.

When I reached the top I stopped to get my breath. It was then that I realised the sun had gone and the air felt wet. I had not gone another twenty yards before the clouds caught up with me. For a few seconds I felt an absurd panic, as the air seemed to choke me. It was like being in the centre of a great ball of wet cotton wool.

Then I remembered Mrs. MacFallor's advice yesterday morning. I sat down to wait.

# CHAPTER SIX

The minutes crept by, but the clouds stood still. Ten minutes, half an hour, one hour, and then it was eleven o'clock and I had left the Grants' croft shortly after nine. Several times I stood up, peered round, edged a tentative foot forward, only to realise how right Mrs. MacFallor had been. I sat down again, shivering. I was now very cold. I thought that if I had to stay put much longer, when the mist finally cleared I should be too stiff to move.

There was little point in worrying about that so I concentrated on Mrs. MacFallor, about whom I was really concerned. I knew that by now she would have guessed what had happened. From her bed she could see the cloud-covered hill on which I sat. I knew she would be very anxious, and I wished hard, as much for her sake as my own, that the wretched mist would blow away.

If only there had been some faint movement in the air, some touch of wind, on which to hang my hopes. There was none at all. The moisture-laden cloud sat heavy and sluggish around me and my hair, face and clothes felt soaking wet.

Twelve o'clock. One. Still no change. Once more I stood up, once more I sat down hopelessly. I was used enough to the thick, yellow London fogs; they were dirty and annoying, but this was something different, something both natural and unnatural. Never before had I been up against the elements like this. I felt extremely puny, extremely insignificant.

The afternoon was well on, and I was past feeling cold. I was a wet bundle of clothes on a mountainside; wet, empty, with no energy left even to feel hungry.

What light there had been was fading. The cloud was very dark, and I could no longer see my watch. In a way this was a relief.

Had they sent anyone to search for me? Was there anyone whom they could send? Angus was booked to take a party fishing on Loch Ardgli, a small sea-loch twenty miles up the coast. The Minister, who was not young himself, would be with his gravely sick mother. Would they contact Hugh? Unlikely, since I knew he had arranged a day's fishing for himself.

He would have been gone long before they would have realised I was lost. I began to shake, not with cold, but with sheer, wild panic. There was no one to come.

I thought again about Hugh. It was something to do. It was very kind of him to have come over yesterday.

I closed my eyes and my cold sleepy brain heard his deep slow voice repeating the words he had used to that girl who had come off a motor-cycle and been in the Theatre on my last morning. 'There,' he had said gently, as if to a child. 'There, don't worry now, it's all over. There is nothing more to be afraid of, my darling.' *My darling?* What was he thinking of? A surgeon in the Theatre, calling a patient *darling*?

And then I discovered that he was not in the

Theatre, that there was no patient, that I was not still drifting in my frightened dreams, that I was hearing his voice here, now.

I tried to sit up, and I felt someone's arms about me. I said, 'Am I awake?' I did not really expect an answer.

His arms tightened round me and my head dropped on his shoulder. It was wonderful not to be alone any longer. I felt absurdly safe and secure. Absurdly, because the fog was still there. But it did not worry me. I did not know how, or when, we'd get home. I only knew it was not my problem now. I was safe with Hugh Sanders.

'Thank heavens I've found you at last,' he said. His voice was soothing.

And then I did a stupid thing. I wept on his shoulder.

'I'm sorry, Hugh,' I said when I stopped. 'It's just that it's such a relief.'

'I don't mind,' he said. 'And, anyway, what is a shoulder for?'

I sniffed unromantically.

'I suppose you haven't such a thing as a dry handkerchief on you? Everything I have is wringing wet.'

I could not see his face, but I knew from his voice that he was smiling.

'I come in handy if purely for utilitarian purposes,' he murmured. 'Yes, I think I have a dry handkerchief. I'm fairly wet myself, but my coat is thicker than yours.' He moved one arm and fumbled in a pocket, still holding on to me with the other arm.

'What are you doing up here in this fog?' I asked when I had dealt with my face.

He laughed outright.

'My dear girl, what do you think I was doing? Looking for you of course! Now,' his face was close to mine, 'are you all right for a moment? Because I've got something for you.'

'I'm all right,' I said shakily. 'But how did you know I was stuck? And how did you manage to find me at all?'

'Radar,' he said. Then he laughed again. 'No, it's not fair to tease you! Just give me your hand, here, and drink this –'

'What's this?'

He switched on a small medical pocket-torch. The light hung round the glass bulb and only penetrated a few inches of fog. I saw the flask in his hand.

He said, 'Take it, and have some.'

'What is it?' I repeated.

'Whisky. Come along.'

I said, 'I don't like it, thanks. No.'

'Don't be infantile, Clare! This isn't exactly a social occasion. If ever anyone was a case for whisky, you are now. Drink up.'

'I'm sorry,' I apologised meekly and did as I was told.

'I did not mean to bully you,' he said as I returned the flask.

The drink was warming me already. I felt more normal.

'How did you know? Did Ailsa telephone?' I asked.

'I met that ghillie, Angus Grant, early this morning,' he said. 'He told me about your doings in the night. Congratulations.'

'I didn't do much,' I said truthfully.

He said dryly, 'You merely brought a child safely into the world.' As I made no answer he went on, 'I thought I would walk over and drop in on your patient again.'

'I thought you had booked a day's fishing?'

'It wasn't settled. There was some hold-up over a boat. I got to Mrs. MacFallor's as they were finishing a late breakfast. They could see the mist coming your way by then, and Mrs. MacFallor was getting anxious.

So I suggested coming to find you. And I did.'

'But that was this morning. Early.'

'Well,' he said in that same dry tone, 'this has been quite a foggy day. I'm afraid I couldn't go very fast.'

'I couldn't go at all. How did you manage?'

'Mostly on all-fours,' he said. 'I must have made a wonderful spectacle, but it was the only safe way for an amateur. Anyway, does it matter? I found you, that's the main thing.'

'Yes.' I realised I was still leaning against his shoulder. I drew away slightly. 'What are we going to do now?'

He did not answer my question. He said briefly, 'Are you uncomfortable?'

I said quickly, 'No, just a bit stiff. The result of sitting in one place all day.'

'Lie back on the grass for a second and stretch out. It's warmer that way.' Then he asked casually, 'Are you cold?'

'Frozen! My blood turned to ice hours ago. Hasn't yours?'

He said nothing for a moment and I felt rather than saw him moving. 'Now sit up, Clare. Here, slip your arms into this.'

I discovered that, gently but firmly, I was being pushed into his tweed jacket. I sat bolt upright. 'Thank you, but no. I wouldn't dream of it.'

'This is no dream,' he said amicably. 'Put it on and don't argue, like a good girl!'

'We are both cold,' I said, 'and the reason you are cold is because you were looking for me! I refuse to let you catch pneumonia on top of everything else! Thank you very much for the kind thought, and thank you very, very much for finding me. But I will not wear your jacket.'

He sat very still, and I thought that was the end of the episode, until he said calmly, 'Under normal conditions I wouldn't consider forcing you to do something against your will, but up here I haven't a scruple. Either you stop fussing and wear my jacket, or I put it on you. And when it comes to brute force,' he sounded almost bored, 'do I have to remind you that I'm bigger and stronger than you?'

'Oh,' was all I said as I slipped into his warm jacket.

We sat in silence for several minutes. I had to grip my teeth to keep them still. My whole body was shaking with cold. Quite suddenly all my fears came back.

'Hugh,' I whispered, 'what are we going to do? How much longer will this mist last, do you think?'

He said cheerfully, 'Well, we are not going to perish miserably on this wretched hillside.'

'You think we can get down?' I peered into the black blanket that seemed thicker than ever. I could not see that we had any hope of moving, but he sounded capable of anything.

He said, 'It's not really as late as one thinks. Could you find the torch? It's in the inside pocket of that thing you're wearing.' (I found it for him and he focused it on his wrist-watch.) 'It's only ten now.'

'So we just go on sitting here?' I said when we had settled again.

'I'm afraid so. I don't know this part of the country at all, nor do you, and we'd be going down, which is far more dangerous. It leaves us no option. It took me nearly nine hours to find you; I can't say that I fancy another lengthy stroll, even could we guarantee that we'd be strolling in the right direction.'

'But it might go on for days!' I said stupidly.

'Well, if it does,' he said amusedly, 'just think of the fun they'll have at Augustine's, when you and I are headlined in the morning papers! It's really almost worth it to visualise the sensation it would cause in our immediate circle.'

I laughed weakly.

'I'm sorry about Bill, Clare,' he said a little while later. He sounded very tired.

'Thanks,' I said. 'But it's all right – or almost all right now.'

He said, 'You're a shocking liar, my dear.'

'Well, what else is there to say?' I asked, and he did not answer.

'I suppose it was inevitable when you think of Sheila Mandin,' I added unthinkingly. 'She's so very much more his type. She's witty and so wonderfully attractive.'

'And you're not?' His voice was strangely sad.

'Would I be here?' I asked more bitterly than I could have wished. 'Would I be sitting here, in this fog, if I were?' I pulled myself together as I remembered how he, too, must be feeling about Sheila, if Jenny, Angie and even Sister Theatre were right. (Sister Theatre was always right about everything.) 'Everything is such a mess all round.'

He said quietly, 'I'm not sure that we are talking about the same thing, but the answer's the same. It's all right. You're a one-man girl, and I'm a one-girl man, so I've discovered in the past few months. We've both been unlucky. That's all there is to it.'

We were both quiet after that, and in the silence I realised I was almost warm.

And then I thought how good it was of Hugh to have taken all that trouble finding me, how well he was looking after me, how comfortable and reassuring his presence was.

It was absurd to feel as safe as I now did, since

Hugh was as lost as I. But absurd or not, that was how I felt. In a little while I fell asleep.

I woke suddenly some time later, and could not think where I was.

Then, as it all came back, with the full knowledge of my surroundings, I realised something else. Hugh's face was resting lightly on my cheek.

He must have dozed off, too. I was glad for him. He had been so thoughtful and cheerful, but he must have been desperately tired. I opened my eyes carefully, to look at the fog. I did not want to disturb him unnecessarily.

The mist was still there, thick as ever. I must have moved my head unconsciously, because as I looked up, his face lifted quickly from mine. He was not asleep.

'Any hope?' I asked.

He said flatly, 'None at all. Have you had a good sleep?'

'Yes, thanks.' I sat up and he dropped his arms heavily to his sides. 'I'm afraid I've given you cramp,' I said.

'I think I hear –' He pushed me gently away, jumped up, and yelled into the darkness, 'Hallo! Here!'

He yelled again. His voice came back to us, alone. He called a third time, and the sound returned, and then we heard another voice.

Ten minutes later Angus Grant with his brother-in-law, Tom Christie, reached us. An hour and a half later we were all back in the big kitchen in Kreagh House, drinking hot, sweet cocoa in front of the fire, and being petted and spoiled by Ailsa, Janet and Gilly.

Mrs. MacFallor was awake and had been told of our return. But Ailsa would not allow us upstairs until we had been warmed and fed.

'You'll mind that you dry yourself off first, Sister dear, and you, too, Doctor. The Mistress is well content to bide a while, now she knows you are safe. She is not wanting you to take your death of cold by staying wet as you are a minute longer than is necessary.'

She rounded on Hugh, who stood with his back to one corner of the glowing peat fire.

'Aye, you young gentlemen are all alike! Though you'll forgive me saying a doctor should have had more thought! You should have waited, Doctor, for me to give you sandwiches. You must be famished.'

'I should have indeed,' Hugh smiled down at her.

'Did you miss lunch, too?' I asked, surprised. 'I thought you were certain to have had food with you, and have eaten it on the way.'

'Really, Clare! Did you seriously imagine that I had been guzzling sandwiches on the hillside, when I knew you were lost and unfed?'

I blushed as they all looked at me. 'I'm sorry. I wasn't thinking.'

'Guzzling!' Janet snorted over the fried eggs she was cooking. 'And not even a bap would the Doctor be taking with him in his hurry to be away.'

'Sister doesn't credit it,' said Hugh lightly. 'Sister has a poor opinion of my unfortunate self.'

'Hugh,' I remonstrated. 'Hugh, please.'

He put his hands in his pockets and rocked on his heels. 'A fact,' he informed them with a grin, and the way they all smiled back showed that they thought he was joking.

I watched him, chatting to Janet, teasing Gilly, being fussed over by Ailsa; the three old women behaved as if they had known him for years. Perhaps they were right, in a way. They certainly knew him better than I did. With 'the girls', and on the way home with Angus and Tom, he had been relaxed and cheerful. There was no trace of his usual remote attitude to people who were not his patients.

The odd thing was that he seemed so normal this way. It seemed right and proper that we should all be laughing together in this friendly kitchen, after the terrible day. I wondered suddenly about his own home. Where did he come from? What was his family? It's amazing how little you can know of your colleagues' backgrounds, in any large establishment like a hospital, with the exception of the half-dozen or so great friends that you made over the years.

I thought, 'He must come from a home like mine. This is how our boys behave.' Of course, they were all a good deal younger than Hugh, but Hugh was reminding me of them now. My elder brother who was a year younger than myself was shy and quiet in public. People who did not know him well called him 'stand-offish'. I was surprised that I had never before noticed that Mark was very like Hugh.

Hugh had seen me looking at him, he was looking back, and something in his expression made me drop my eyes.

I stood up. 'I'm warm now, Ailsa. I think I'll just run up to Mrs. MacFallor, before I eat Janet's eggs.'

Hugh said, 'Do you think she'd care to see me? Or shall I wait here?'

'No, you come, too.'

'My dear child,' said Mrs. MacFallor gently, 'my dear, I'm so happy to see you back.'

I bent down and kissed her soft cheek. 'I'm so happy to be here, and so sorry you should have had all this anxiety.'

'I have been very anxious,' she said, 'but not as

anxious as I should have been if I had thought you were alone.'

'You guessed Mr. Sanders would find me?'

Her blue eyes smiled. 'I prayed,' she said simply, 'and I knew he would.' She looked beyond me at him. 'Such a comfort,' she said. 'It was such a comfort that you were here, Mr. Sanders. But I mustn't take all the credit for my faith, Mr. Sanders. I also used my judgement.'

'You thought I was capable of penetrating that mist?'

She closed her tired, young-old eyes, 'No.' She opened them again and looked steadily at him. 'I recognise a determined young man when I see one.'

Hugh bowed his head slightly. 'Thank you, Mrs. MacFallor,' he said quietly.

It was past one in the morning when I finally dropped into bed, too tired for sleep. I lay and watched the darkness that was now a friend and not an enemy. My mind went round and round in circles, as I went over the day, the evening, the welcome here, Mrs. MacFallor's words; whether Hugh was sleeping, or whether he, too, was awake in Sir Inister's room where Mrs. MacFallor and 'the girls' had insisted he stay tonight.

'Lucky Sheila,' I thought suddenly. 'Lucky, lucky Sheila. To inspire love in two men like Bill and Hugh. Where did I go wrong?'

To cheer myself up, I reminded myself that there was always Andrew. He was not serious, but he was fun, and at least he liked me. I was lucky, too. I dozed off eventually. Half-way through what was left of the night I had to turn my pillow over because it was wet with tears.

***

Jilly brought in a letter with my tea next morning. 'It came last afternoon, Sister, but I was too worried to charge my memory with it in the night.'

The letter was from Jenny.

'*All kinds of things are going on here, Clare! First, I must tell you one simply enormous bit of gossip. Do you know who our new Surgical Registrar really is? My dear, it appears he's THE Andrew Wells-Darvie! You know, Wells-Darvie biscuits. Think of that! We've never had a millionaire operating in our Theatre before. Sister's tickled pink, although, of course, she hasn't said so. Apparently he's furious, as he's really keen on his job and wanted to be incog. I suppose that's why he crossed the river. The hospital is ablaze with it. One of the Private Patients let the cat among the pigeons. And do you need three guesses to discover who is going round with a lost expression and a flashing smile? You're right. Our old friend Sheila. She's got her eye on Darvie now, has Sheila. Of course she's still officially engaged to Bill, but I've no doubt she reasons that as that didn't stop Bill, why should it stop her? Which Mike says may be called retribution. I wouldn't know. But what I do know is that I wouldn't say your ex-fiancé has much of a hope if he's in competition with the Wells-Darvie fortune!*'

Hugh left the next morning. He was summoned back to the hospital. We had been sitting at breakfast, comparing the various aches we had acquired during those hours on the hill, when the telephone-bell rang. The call was for Hugh. It had been put through from the hotel. Mike Gill, Jenny's fiancé and the Senior Surgical Registrar at Augustine's, announced that Sir Inister had gone down with a chest infection. Sir Inister had not wanted Hugh to be recalled, but Mike

Gill had told him he knew Hugh well enough to know he'd prefer to be told.

Hugh said, 'Of course you had to tell me, Mike. I'll start back in a couple of hours.'

Mike said he was sorry to have spoilt Hugh's fishing.

Hugh said briefly, 'That's all right. Thanks for letting me know. Give my regards to Sir Inister.' Then he added seriously, 'Just how bad is he?'

I learned later that Mike had said: 'Bad enough to be in bed, and exuding charm to one and all. He needs a long holiday. Who doesn't in this game?'

'Well, thanks for ringing,' said Hugh. 'See you some time tomorrow evening, Mike.'

He replaced the receiver slowly and stood with his back to me for a few seconds, looking out of the window. Then he turned and as his back was to the light I could not see the expression on his face as he told me what Mike had said.

'Sir Inister has had far too much chest trouble lately for my liking,' I said.

'He's getting on,' Hugh agreed, 'and he won't spare himself, so Nature revenges herself. I'm afraid he must be really bad to have allowed himself to be hospitalised. Usually, the most I can persuade him to do is to take a day or two off in his club.'

I refilled our tea-cups. 'But you've had no holiday at all, what with your social calling on the first day and your wild-goose chase for me yesterday.' I was stricken with remorse. 'I am sorry to have made you waste all that time.'

'I wouldn't say it was a waste of time.' Then when he saw I did not understand, he added, 'You had to be found, Clare.'

I smiled. 'I suppose I did! But I'm still sorry that it

had to be you.'

'Are you?' It was an ordinary question, but his voice was strange. I glanced at him quickly. He was not looking at me; he was again staring out of the window.

'Do you know,' he said, 'for the first time in my life I can raise no enthusiasm at all at the prospect of getting back to work.' He smiled at me. 'What do you think's wrong? Am I getting lazy?'

I pushed back my chair. 'I doubt it. I don't think anyone could call you that.' I stood up. 'I must go and see if Mrs. MacFallor is awake yet.' Then I hesitated. 'What shall I tell her about you? I don't want her to worry over Sir Inister.'

'No, we don't want to do that,' he said. 'We'll have to think up something near the truth. I don't care to lie to people, but I can't see any good coming out of our explaining the real situation.'

'Shall we stick to the truth as far as possible?' I said. 'I'll say that you've gone back because you've heard there's a special case coming on for which they'll need your assistance? She'll understand your breaking your holiday for that. She knows how you feel about your job.'

He raised an eyebrow.

'I'm afraid I'm guilty,' I said. 'I've been nattering to her about my life in the Theatre.'

He said mildly, 'Do I come in under that heading?'

'Of course.'

He nodded. 'What does Mrs. MacFallor say about it all?'

I shrugged. 'Nothing special. She's interested but then she's interested in everything.' As I spoke I did remember something Mrs. MacFallor had said about him. The thought must have shown on my face, because he said:

'Perhaps you were wise to work in the Theatre. Your mask is your defence, Clare. Without it, your face gives you away. What else did she say?'

I looked down at him for a second or two before I answered, 'She said she thought you hid not only your face but your feelings behind a mask.'

He neither smiled, nor made some light remark, as I had expected. Instead, he said nothing at all, and his face was blank. I was certain that I had annoyed him, and after his kindness to me last night, I did not want to do that. 'Would you mind pouring me out another cup of tea?' I asked quickly.

'With pleasure.' He reached for the teapot. 'But I thought you were off upstairs?'

'I must go and see if she's awake,' I said. 'But I'm pretty certain she won't be after her late night. In which case I'd like to join you in another cup. Remember I'm a nurse, Doctor. And no right-minded nurse can leave a teapot until it's completely empty.'

'No right-minded surgeon, either, Nurse Maitland!'

We laughed together and the moment of strain was gone.

'You nip up,' he said, 'then you'll be back sooner and we can sit over the remains of the breakfast. If this is to be the last morning of my holiday, I want to enjoy it. I hate rushed meals.'

'Poor Hugh,' I turned in the doorway. 'You're in the wrong set-up, in that case.'

He glanced slowly round the room, then back to me. 'There's nothing much wrong with this set-up, Clare. In fact it's almost perfect.'

'That wasn't exactly what I meant.'

He said, 'I know. I also know what you meant. And it isn't the set-up that's to blame. I'm the one that is out of place.'

'Hugh,' I said on an impulse, 'I'm so very sorry for you – about Bill and Sheila, I mean.'

His expression changed. 'Bill Blake and Sheila Mandin?'

'Yes,' I said quickly, before my courage ran out. 'I do know how you are feeling.'

'Do you, Clare?' he asked gently.

'Yes.' I gripped the door-handle for support. I half-smiled. 'It's not much fun, is it? Loving someone who is already in love with someone else?'

He said, 'It isn't, is it?'

Then I went out quickly and shut the door quietly behind me.

Mrs. MacFallor was still asleep. I had a whispered word with Gilly on the landing, and told her to let Janet know that Mr. Sanders was returning to London that day.

'Janet will be sad to hear it, Sister, as she was thinking the Doctor would be having a fine luncheon before returning to the hotel.'

'I doubt that he'll get lunch anywhere, beyond sandwiches,' I said. 'He's got a lot of miles to cover in the next twenty-four hours.'

'Does he have to be going back, Sister?'

'He does, I'm afraid, Gilly.'

Gilly shook her head and said a doctor's life was aye a hard one, then pottered slowly downstairs again to break the news to Janet and Ailsa.

Hugh had put my cup of tea on the hot-plate. 'I'm glad you weren't long. I was afraid I'd crack the cup. Is it still hot?'

'It's just right, thanks. And thank you very much for heating this. It was very thoughtful of you.'

'I told you last night that I was good for purely

utilitarian purposes.' He grinned. I sat down again and he did the same.

'I must admit that just before you arrived I decided I was not long for this world,' I said. 'But then I fell asleep and did not wake until you broke into my Theatre nightmare. I remember what brought me down to earth with a bang was the idea of a surgeon calling a patient –' I stopped, embarrassed.

'My darling?' he suggested calmly.

I nodded.

'My dear Clare,' he said, and for the first time since his arrival here he looked and sounded like the Mr. Sanders who was a Master of Surgery and First Assistant to Sir Inister MacFallor. 'Foggy hills have a strangely primitive effect upon me. Please do not remind me of my own weakness. That's something over which I, too, would like to draw a veil.'

It was quite unreasonable of me, but I felt as if he had slapped my face. In the silence that followed, all our new friendship seemed to slip away, and the old, strained atmosphere that I had always felt with him in the past crept back. I finished my tea quickly. 'I'd better get back upstairs. Mrs. MacFallor may wake up any time now.'

He said formally, 'Will you thank her for putting me up? And tell her how sorry I am not to say good-bye?'

'Of course.' I asked if he were walking back to the hotel.

He said, 'No. I rang them while you were upstairs. They are sending a car over for me. I don't want to waste any time in getting off. I'd like to do as many of those six hundred miles as I can by daylight.'

***

A quarter of an hour later the hotel car arrived. My patient was still sleeping, so I went down to the front hall again, where Ailsa, Janet and Gilly had clustered to see Hugh go.

'The Mistress will be grieving not to have seen you, Doctor,' said Ailsa. 'But she will aye be grateful to you for finding Sister. Haste ye back.'

'Aye,' echoed old Janet severely, 'haste ye back, Doctor. It was a good day, the day you were deciding to come to Loch Kreagh for your holiday.'

'It won't be this year, I'm afraid,' he said, as he shook their hands in turn. 'I left it a bit late as it was. Let's hope next time I can stay longer.'

They beamed up at him as if he were a long-lost nephew.

'Goodbye, Clare.' He held out his hand to me.

'Goodbye,' I said. 'And thank you very much for stumbling into me at the right moment.'

He said, 'Was that what I did?'

'Well, didn't you?' I glanced up at his face; there was an odd expression in his eyes, which I understood no more than I understood what he meant by his question.

He said, 'I should have said it was hardly the right moment. I'm afraid it took me a long time to find you.' His voice was very deep. 'Too long.' He looked down at my hand which he was still holding. He seemed almost surprised to see it, as if he had forgotten all about that particular handclasp. I moved my fingers slightly and he let them go at once …

# CHAPTER SEVEN

'Are there any messages you want delivered?' Hugh asked me abruptly.

'Messages?' I remembered the last time he had said that to me. That night when I had asked him to give the letter returning my ring to Bill. He surely could not be so cruel as to do that intentionally? Then I realised that, of course, he had never known what was in that package. His next words proved this, as he said casually: 'Yes. For Sister Theatre, or Nurse Evans, or your friend –' his voice lingered on the word – 'Darvie?'

'Oh. Oh, yes. Give them my love and tell them I look forward to seeing them all again.'

'To all of them?' he queried politely.

'Yes, of course, all of them!'

The car wound its way round the loch, then disappeared over the bend of the first hill. The three old women shivered and went slowly indoors.

I went up to Mrs. MacFallor, who had not woken. I had nothing to do for the moment, so I went to my own room. There were a good many things I could attend to there; letters that needed writing, my own mending, the sock I was knitting for one of the boys, a crochet shawl for Mrs. MacFallor's birthday. I did none of these things. I sat down at my writing-desk and stared out of the window at the loch. I did not see the loch at all. I saw the smoke-grimed walls of the hospital and I ached, in a suddenly overwhelming wave of homesickness, to be back. I longed for the faint clean scent of ether and iodoform that was always there in the air. Above all, I longed for the rush of work, the incessant demands of my job.

I took out Jenny's last letter and reread it. From what Jenny wrote, it would seem that Bill – my Bill – might be free again. And if he were free, he might need me. Well then, wasn't that what I had been wanting, all these past lonely months? It was, I thought soberly, it was. And then I knew what was wrong. I had used the past tense. And that was where my love for Bill had gone – into the past …

I put my head down on my arms. 'Oh, no. Not again. I can't go through it all again.'

At that I was really annoyed with myself. This was just the result of that stupid fog yesterday, and the wonderful sensation of relief, comfort, and security I had felt in Hugh's arms. And the owner of those arms was now driving back to London and Sheila, the girl he loved. A girl who, according to Jenny, was soon to be free of her engagement to Bill.

Jenny might say Sheila was determined to catch Andrew Darvie; Mrs. MacFallor had said Hugh was a determined young man. And I had known Jenny to be mistaken over things before. The more I saw of Mrs. MacFallor, the more I realised she was the wisest person I had ever met.

What was it Andrew had said to me when he heard

I was going away? '*Be careful you don't step out of the frying-pan into the fire.*'

It was my first day back at the hospital. The telephone on the duty-room desk rang twice. Sister Theatre put her head round the glove-room door.

'Would you take that for me, Nurse Maitland? I must get away to Matron's office with my off-duty list, or there'll be ructions!'

'Yes, Sister.' I shot into the duty-room and picked up the jingling instrument. 'Operating Theatre here. Staff Nurse speaking.'

'Mr. Sanders speaking,' said Hugh's voice briefly. 'Nurse Evans, would you please tell Sister that Sir Inister is going to be late? His car has broken down, and he's just rung to say he's coming on by train. We'll be able to start at eleven. And would you also tell Sister that I'm sorry this is going to mean all of us working through lunch. I'm afraid there's no alternative.'

I glanced at the list that was pinned to the wall as he spoke. I saw the name of the first of the day's head cases. Roughly four hours, I guessed. The prospect of missing lunch would not worry Sister or any of us, I knew. What suited Sir Inister suited his Theatre staff.

I said, 'Thank you, Mr. Sanders. I'll tell Sister as soon as she gets back from the office. Shall we let the ward know? Or has your house-surgeon done that?'

There was silence, and I thought we had been cut off. I touched the receiver-rest, and heard the voice of the porter on the switchboard, 'You wanting me, Nurse Maitland?'

'Please, Thomas. Can you reconnect me with Mr. Sanders? We seem to have been cut off.'

'Right you are, Nurse.'

Hugh said, 'No, we aren't cut off, Nurse Maitland.

And yes, the house-surgeon has told the ward.'

'Nurse thought she had lost you, sir,' said Thomas cheerfully.

'No.' Hugh sounded amused. 'Nurse hasn't done that.' He waited for Thomas to get off the line. 'You still there, Nurse?'

I said I was.

'When did you get back? I thought the boss was bringing you with him this morning?'

'He was, but he had to see an emergency in Doncaster yesterday. He wasn't happy about the case, so he decided to stay there a few more hours and I did the rest by train.'

'I see.' He asked after Mrs. MacFallor and 'the girls'.

I said I had left them safely in Miss Davidson's care.

'I expect they'll miss you. Have you promised to return?'

'Just as soon as I can afford the fare!'

He said, 'You really liked it up there, didn't you?'

'Yes.'

'Well –' he hesitated – 'it's nice to know you are back in the Theatre. Sorry about this morning's hold-up, but it's just one of those things.'

'Of course. Thank you for letting us know.'

His words reminded me of something Bill had once said. I smiled wryly at the recollection as I replaced the receiver. It was nice for me, too, to know they were both glad I was in the Theatre.

Jenny bustled into the duty-room. 'What was all that about, Clare? And wherefore the enigmatic smile?'

I told her about the change in times, then added: 'And Mr. Sanders was being civil and saying he was glad I was back.'

Jenny chuckled. 'Then I'm not surprised at your smile, knowing what you think of him.' (*Did she?*)

'I'll tell you someone else who's glad you are back, and that's Jane Innes. Poor dear, she has had a ghastly time with our men. She hasn't been able to do a thing right for any of them. Sir Inister has kept up a running "Nurse Maitland never bothered me with foolish questions!" Andy Darvie has smiled sweetly and said, "Well, well, we can't all be born Theatre Staff Nurses", and your pet aversion has said nothing but looked so out-of-this-worldish, dreaming about Sheila, I suppose, all the time you've been away that he's reminded me of you last August.' Jenny unbuckled her belt and pulled off her apron as she talked. 'I've often thought a little unrequited love is good for the young men,' she said thoughtfully. 'But it's hard on the Theatre staff!'

'Jenny, who are you talking about now?'

'Mr. Sanders, of course. Who else? You don't imagine dear old Sir Inister has suddenly gone barmy, do you? And as for Andy Darvie, he's not the type to love in vain!'

'Is Sheila's engagement to Bill really over?'

She looked at me oddly as she untied her cap strings. 'Did you see much of Mr. Sanders in Scotland?'

'He was only up for a couple of days.' I avoided her question as she had mine.

She said casually, 'Did you see Angie Shane or any of your set last evening?'

'No.' I untied my own cap. 'Angie's off for three days, and the others were on-duty.'

'Well,' she said slowly. 'I don't know how you feel about things now, Clare, even if you are still interested. But personally I always think it's a good thing for a girl to know what's going on. You remember that letter I wrote you?'

'Which one? You wrote several.' Then I dropped pretence. 'Jenny, are you trying to tell me something about Bill?'

'You know that the wedding date was to be at the end of this month?'

I said Angie had told me.

'Well, Sheila is now wandering round the hospital saying that November is a perfectly grim month for a wedding, don't we agree, my dears?' Jenny flickered her eyes in a perfect reproduction of Sheila's pet mannerism. 'The long and short of it is that Bill has gone off to the wilds as a G.P., and dear Sheila has had a natter with Matron and decided to remain here until the end of the year. I must say,' continued Jenny grimly, 'I should like to have been a fly on the wall at that interview! I'll bet Matron said plenty, although of course she wouldn't chuck Sheila out for absconding with your young man. For all her charms, Sheila is a good girl at her job. And also Matron, whom, as we all know, is no fool, may think it'll teach Bill Blake a sharp lesson. Which he needs.'

'Is their engagement really over, Jenny?' I held my breath as I waited for her answer. I held my breath but not for the reason Jenny might have expected.

'Yes and no. She's still wearing Bill's ring. I imagine because it's pretty. But there's a new man. Not Sanders, he's got no cash. It's Andy.'

I opened my mouth to say something, thought better of it, and tied a mask over my face instead.

'That's right!' said Jenny cheerfully, as if I had spoken. 'All the money in the world. Just as I foretold.'

'But Andrew knows she's engaged to Bill.'

'Of course he knows. Everyone knows.'

'I'm a little surprised at Andrew,' I said.

'You'll be still more surprised when you see them together then,' said Jenny. 'Me, I think Andy's being very naughty. I may be wrong, and I know Sheila's got a way with her. But I think she's met her equal. Andy obviously reckons nothing to her future plans with Bill Blake, and is just enjoying life and the sweet smiles of the prettiest girl in the hospital. And he's got something there, because Sheila really is lovely.'

'And Hugh Sanders?'

Jenny had settled her Theatre turban; now she turned to look at me. 'You're very concerned with that young man, Clare. I thought you loathed the sight of him.'

I said conversationally, 'He was awfully nice to my patient in Scotland. He showed me a slightly different side of his character. And, like Sister, I'm rather sorry for him.'

'Did Sister say that?'

I nodded.

'She's probably right,' Jenny went on. 'I expect the reason you are now feeling charitable is that having been badly hurt yourself, you have a fellow feeling for someone in the same spot.'

'Yes.' I was glad of my mask. 'You think he's very upset?'

'Well, it must be that,' said Jenny. 'He's so odd. So different. Mike says he remembers him as a houseman. He was never like this. Quiet, yes – but merry and bright at the same time. Now he just says nothing.' Sister came back from the office then and we told her of the change-over.

'I'm sorry you've had to dress-up, Nurse Maitland. In view of what's happening, you had better change again. We've got a long general surgical list to fit in this afternoon, and it will have to be done in the annexe – although what Mr. Hedley will say about that I do not know! I imagine he'll be furious. He does so dislike being done out of his audience in the gallery. You'll have to calm him as best you can, Nurse Maitland.'

'Me, Sister?'

'You, Nurse.' Her eyebrows danced. 'You look strong enough for anything, after your sojourn in the hills. Even if you did get lost in a fog!'

'Sister! How did you know?'

'I heard two versions of the story,' said Sister placidly. 'One from Sir Inister, who heard it from Mr. Sanders, and one from Mr. Sanders himself. I can't wait to hear yours. You must tell me about it when we next have occasion to polish instruments together. Now you had better get off-duty, and come back at twelve-thirty. I anticipate a somewhat hectic day after this quiet start.'

Jenny's large brown eyes gleamed expressively over her white mask. Sister's back was to her at that moment and she winked deliberately.

'Polish instruments with me sometime, Clare,' she murmured, as she flashed past me on her way into the Theatre.

None of my particular friends was off-duty that morning. I had finished all my unpacking the night before, written a short note to my old friends in Scotland telling them I had arrived safely; and a longer letter to my family, saying I was back in London. I changed out of uniform and wondered what to do with my two hours. I did not want to hang about in the Home or round the hospital. I felt strangely restless. I decided to go for a walk.

I went quickly down the front steps of the Nurses'

Home and then turned left, along the road that led directly to the heart of the dockland and the river. There was a special lane and a seat at the head of a flight of muddy river stairs, that through the years had become almost hospital property. I had not been near either that lane or that seat since that August afternoon when I had had Bill's letter. In the old days that was our favourite spot for strolling, and on that seat we had talked and planned our future. I walked thoughtfully down the narrow lane, which was lined with long sad rows of grey warehouses, smelling of tar and rope and river smoke. It had been raining earlier this morning, and their roofs still dropped slow, heavy tears on to myself and the other passers-by Two men, in working overalls, walked past on the other side of the lane. They glanced incuriously my way, and although I was in mufti murmured, ''Morning, Nurse,' with the sixth sense that all Londoners and seamen in that part of the world seemed to possess.

'Good morning,' I answered and walked on.

I had reached the head of the lane and the top of the river steps without realising it. A man was sitting on the seat with his back to me. At the sound of my steps he glanced over his shoulder. We recognised each other at the same moment. I stood quite still and watched Bill stand up slowly.

'Clare,' he said simply, 'are you real? Or am I seeing things? I thought you were in the Highlands?' He came forward quickly and took my hands.

'Hullo, Bill.' I found I could say no more. My heart was thumping so loudly that he must hear it.

He said, 'Come and sit down, Clare.' Still holding my hand, he led me to the stone seat. He laughed nervously. 'You are sure you're real? Quite sure?

Because I still can't believe it.'

I had myself well in hand now. 'Why? After all, I walked around here for years before I met you. This is one of my oldest haunts. I should have thought you might well have expected to see me here.'

'Don't be silly!' he said impatiently. 'You know quite well what I mean. We used to come here in the old days. Somehow I didn't feel that you would ever come here again.'

'I never have, until today.'

'Why today?'

I turned the question. 'Why are you here? I didn't even know you were in London.'

'I'll explain that in a moment,' he said briefly. 'But I want to know more about you. You still haven't answered my question. And when did you get back from that ghastly place?'

'What ghastly place?' I moved my hands from his gently. 'You can't mean Loch Kreagh? It wasn't ghastly, Bill. It was perfect, and I loved it there.'

He shook his head in obvious disbelief. 'Why did you go?' he asked curtly.

I sighed. 'To get away from you.'

'And why have you come back? Because you knew I had left? Or because of –' his gaze left my face and he looked at the ground – 'because of something you had heard?'

'I came back because the job was over. That's all.'

He kicked at a small stone with one foot. 'Would you have come back if I had still been in the hospital?'

I said dryly, 'Why not? It wouldn't have been the first time we had worked together – unengaged.'

'Clare!' His voice was reproachful. 'This isn't like you.'

I shrugged. 'I'm sorry. Maybe I've changed a good bit lately.'

'Not you, too, Care,' he said quickly. 'I couldn't bear that!'

Bill's shoulders were hunched, almost defeated. I felt a rush of sympathy for him. 'What's gone wrong?' I said gently.

He did not turn his face to look at me, as he answered, 'Just about everything. Didn't you know?' His voice was now as dry as mine had been. 'What's upset the hospital grape-vine? It was always up to the minute in my day.'

'I haven't been back long,' I explained. 'In fact, I only got back last night. I haven't had a chance to hear much gossip.'

Now he looked at me. 'All the same, you have heard something.'

'Yes.'

'What?'

I shook my head. 'Gossip is never worth repeating or remembering.'

'Perhaps you can tell we whether I am still engaged to Sheila? I came up this morning to talk things over. She asked me to come. I imagine at least half the hospital must know she has asked me. I've attached myself to a very chatty young woman.'

'Bill, stop!' ('Oh, Sheila,' I thought, 'What have you done to him, to make him talk this way?') 'You mustn't say things like that. Not about her. Not to me, or anyone else. You're still engaged.'

'Am I?' he asked cynically. 'Hasn't Darvie proposed? My position seems to hang on that.'

I stared at him. What was wrong with everyone? People, ordinary, normal, decent people, did not behave like that.

'But he can't. Not while she's engaged to you.'

'My dear,' he murmured, 'you're very sweet, and very out of date. Do you really set such store by a ring with a few stones attached?'

I thought, 'This is where we went wrong. This is where Bill and I would always go wrong. We speak a different language in the same tongue.'

I was still staring at him as if he were a stranger. I said, 'I do set store on what that particular ring means.'

He looked at me for a long time, then his gaze dropped again. 'I'm sorry, Clare. I deserved that. Did I hurt you terribly?'

Pride should have made me pretend. As I have never quite seen where pride fits in with love, I answered honestly, 'More than I would have known it was possible to be hurt.'

He still did not look up. 'Is there anything I can do?'

'Why?'

Now he turned to me. 'Clare, don't you understand? It's been just an infatuation! A stupid, foolish, criminal infatuation on my part. I couldn't help myself, dearest. I do ask you to believe that. I couldn't help myself. And now I've come back to you, to ask you to forgive me, and believe me.'

I had dreamed of Bill saying those words to me: I had dreamed them for weeks, for months.

I said, 'But you did not even know I was in town?'

'What has that to do with it?' he said impatiently. 'The moment I looked round and saw you there behind me. I knew that was what I needed, was to have you behind me always. To come back to.' His voice was calmer now. 'To come home to.'

His last words touched something I had thought dead. Wasn't that, after all, what I, like any other girl, wanted?

I did not answer; I was too moved to speak.

'Would you be willing to try again, Clare? I promise,' he laughed shakily, 'to close my eyes if I see any blondes coming my way!'

His words brought me down to earth with a bump. I had actually forgotten Sheila. 'Bill,' I said, 'you are still engaged. You aren't free to talk to me about this.'

'I told you,' he said, 'she doesn't see this in the same light that you do.'

'But I'm not talking to her. I'm talking to you.' I saw he did not understand so I explained further. 'Supposing that she doesn't want to break it off? Supposing all this wretched talk is just talk? Has she told you herself about Andrew?'

He shrugged. 'She hasn't. I used my eyes before I left, and I've been up here in London a good deal in the last month. These things get about.'

'But you don't know? She might really still be in love with you? I've never known her particularly well, but I should say that Sheila is one of those girls who can't help flirting with every attractive young man she meets. She doesn't mean much harm; it just comes naturally, as naturally as breathing! And I wouldn't have said that Andrew is the marrying type. They might just be passing the time pleasantly.'

A small flame leapt in his eyes. Something that had nothing to do with me. 'Clare, do you really think so?'

'I can't say for sure, because I've seen neither of them for months. But I think you ought to give them the benefit of the doubt. And I'll tell you something else, Bill. You've not been infatuated. You've been – and are – in love.'

'You don't understand, Clare –'

'Listen,' I broke in, 'just listen. If Sheila's still willing to marry you, do you really want me, instead?'

I shot the words at him quickly to take him by surprise. I saw him hesitate.

'You needn't say anything, Bill,' I said. 'I know you don't love me. You only want your hand held. You want a shoulder to weep on.' I stood up. 'No, don't come back with me.' I put my hand on his shoulder and pressed him gently down on to the seat again. 'I want to go alone. I came out here to think, and I still haven't done any thinking. But I have discovered something this morning. So maybe I've accomplished one thing.'

'What's that, my dear?' He tilted his long thin face up to look at me. I knew every line on his face, every expression, by heart.

I looked down at him for a moment before answering. As I looked, I thought, 'This is the last time Bill and I will ever talk like this alone together.' I felt neither happy nor sad. Just empty.

'One is, that when and if I do marry – which I begin to doubt – I don't want to be married because I'm restful, or quiet, or old-fashioned, or anything. I want to be married because I'm me. Goodbye, Bill.'

I turned and walked quickly away down the lane and as I walked I thought about Sheila. It was strange that someone I really knew so little should so affect my life.

Sheila had taken Bill's love from me; Sheila had taken Hugh Sanders' heart, and now she had taken my love for Bill.

It was very hot in the Theatre that afternoon. I did not see Andrew Darvie until he walked into the annexe at a quarter past two, followed by a very irate Mr. Hedley.

Mr. Hedley nodded curtly, ''Afternoon, Nurse.' He

glanced at me a second time and added more civilly, 'Glad to see that Sir Inister has at last dispensed with your services, Nurse Maitland! One would imagine that no other Consultant Surgeon ever worked in this hospital, when one considers how he employs the best nurses for his private affairs and then pushes all other surgery into these corners!'

The annexe was a duplicate of the main Theatre in every respect, excluding its lack of a students' gallery.

Andrew said, ''Afternoon, Nurse Maitland,' and winked behind Mr. Hedley's back as they both walked over to the scrubbing-up sinks.

I murmured something in what I hoped was a soothing manner and went on with my needle-threading.

The first two cases were uneventful. The Theatre grew hotter. My gown, to which in these three months I had grown unaccustomed, felt heavy, and my turban pressed my hair. Mr. Hedley's normally pale face was flaming in the parts visible over his mask; while Andrew's mask was pressed against his nose and cheekbones, as if it had been wrung out in water.

I glanced round for Nurse Martin, my 'dirty' nurse. 'Nurse, Mr Darvie needs the face towel.'

She hurried forward with a clean towel, and Andrew, without moving the position of his hands, twisted his head over his shoulder and leant back slightly, bending his knees as he did so for her to reach up to his face more easily.

Mr. Hedley grunted, 'Might as well do me while you're about it. Nurse. Then he said, 'What's the temperature in here, Nurse Maitland?' I looked over to the thermometer on the wall. 'Eighty-eight.'

He grunted again. 'I want it high for this case. Still, it's fearfully hot.'

I looked at his bent back anxiously. Mr. Hedley was by reputation our Theatre salamander. He never complained of the heat even in midsummer when the combination of the central-heating, lights, and sterilisers, could send the thermometer rocketing. Now, it seemed to me, his shoulders were drooping with something more than his superficial displeasure in having to operate in a gallery-less Theatre.

I tried to catch Andrew's eye, to see whether he had noticed anything wrong, but he did not look up. The anaesthetist was busy with his cylinders, and Nurse Martin was fishing nail-brushes out of their boiling steriliser, when I heard Mr. Hedley sigh. 'Nurse, I want –'

All surgeons say 'I want' at intervals during an operation, without always specifying what it is they do want. Which is why they like to work with a nurse whom they know.

I held out the needle-holder. 'There is nylon on that one, Mr. Hedley.

He said clearly, 'Give it to Mr. Darvie, please, Nurse Maitland,' and collapsed on to the floor at my feet.

My foot had been hovering over the emergency bell. I pressed it three times. The Theatre SOS.

Andrew reached over and took the needle-holder from me. 'Thank you, Nurse,' he said steadily, ignoring Mr. Hedley.

Bows, the porter, was inside the door before the last buzz had died away. 'Mr. Hedley has fainted! Just give a hand there, Nurse Martin.'

Mr. Hedley was a large, heavy man. He was too heavy for thin little Bows and young Nurse Martin to lift alone. The anaesthetist frowned over his mask. 'Sorry I can't give you a hand, but I can't leave this end.'

'Of course not, doctor,' Nurse Martin raised her

flushed face. 'I'm sure we can manage.'

'I don't think you can.' I looked down momentarily. There could be no question of Andrew or myself becoming involved with anyone but our patient. 'Bows, you'll have to get help. Where's Jones?' The other porter.

'He's gone along with that last case of Sir Inister's,' said Bows gloomily. 'I'd best hop into the surgeon's room, Nurse, and see if Mr. Sanders is still there. They've finished next door and I know Sir Inister's gone –'

'You go,' I interrupted. 'And meanwhile, would you get me some more warm saline, please, Nurse Martin?'

Hugh, in shirt-sleeves, a mask and cap hurriedly pulled on, followed Bows into the Theatre a few seconds later.

'I'll take his head,' was all he said, as between them the three of them carried Mr. Hedley from the room.

Nurse Martin returned at once. 'What shall I do, Nurse – stay in here, or outside?'

I handed Andrew the instrument he wanted as I answered, 'Find Nurse Evans quickly. I expect she's having a late lunch in the dining-room. Ring through and ask her to come back. Sister's off. Then you come back in here. Mr. Darvie may want me to assist, as he's one surgeon short.'

Andrew said, 'Not this case. She's all right. Just on finished. But I'll need help with the next, if the old man can't do it.'

Hugh came in again, silently. 'What's the next case, Darvie?'

Andrew explained briefly.

'I'll assist if you like,' said Hugh slowly.

Andrew did not answer for a moment. He finished what he was doing, murmured, 'Bandage, Nurse,' then he straightened and looked at Hugh.

'My good chap, it's after three and you've been at it since eleven. Haven't you had enough? I'll raise the senior house-surgeon.'

'Sister Casualty will probably murder you if you do,' said Hugh cheerfully. 'Bows was just telling me they are as busy as can be there this afternoon. I'm perfectly happy to go on.'

It was the first time I had seen these two men working together. It was interesting to watch their different techniques. Andrew was quick, sure, at times impatient, if the right instrument was not in his hand, or if Hugh was not in the exact position which he, Andrew, required of his assistant. Hugh, as I knew of old, was never in a hurry, never impatient, always certain of himself. One of these days, when he had had more experience, Andrew would be a dramatic surgeon; he had courage, he was afraid of nothing. Hugh would never be dramatic; and since he had greater experience, he knew just how much there was to fear. I had never known Hugh take a risk in the Theatre. I doubted that he ever would; he always knew what he was doing.

Now, although Hugh was Andrew's senior in the hospital hierarchy, he was acting as a junior, and never for one moment did he attempt to be anything else. Andrew ordered what should be done, Hugh and I did as we were told. It was a tricky case.

Andrew put one hand behind him, 'Clamps.'

I put the clamps into his gloved hand. He put them down on the table beside him. 'Think I'll have another ligature first.' Then as he turned his elbow touched the silver clamps and they slid on to the floor

‘For Pete’s sake, Nurse!’ said Andrew impatiently. ‘Watch what you are doing! You’re not in the Highlands now!’

‘I’m sorry, Mr. Darvie,’ I said automatically, and turned to Nurse Martin.

‘There’s another pair in my steriliser. They’re all ready. Would you get them, please?’ Her eyes were indignant as she shot across the Theatre.

‘I have another pair here, Mr. Darvie,’ I said a few seconds later.

‘Well leave ’em on the trolley, Nurse. I’ll pick them up myself when I’m ready. I don’t want anything else thrown on the floor.’

‘Yes, Mr. Darvie,’ I said meekly. I knew my face was scarlet under my mask.

Nurse Martin came and stood by my shoulder. ‘It wasn’t your fault, Nurse,’ she whispered. ‘It had nothing to do with you. You weren’t near them!’

I shook my head slightly to show I did not want to talk. I knew that Andrew was strung-up by his sudden responsibility and that was all that was wrong. I did not mind having to look foolish; no harm had come to the patient, and that was the end of it.

It was not quite the end of it. A second or two later the anaesthetist looked up and caught my eye. He nodded, as if to say, ‘I saw it, too,’ then Hugh, who was standing back from the table, waiting for Andrews next move, deliberately looked my way. He did not smile, but his eyes were extraordinarily kind and understanding.

# CHAPTER EIGHT

When I arrived back from supper that evening, the Theatre was empty.

I settled down at the desk and wrote for a few minutes. Then there was a knock on the open door, and a girl's voice said, 'Are you busy, Maitland? And are you alone? I'd rather like to have a little chat with you.'

Sheila Mandin stood in the doorway, the pristine fairness of her hair and skin making the general effect quite staggering …

I looked up. 'I'm not busy, Sheila, and I'm quite alone. Come in and sit down.'

Sheila Mandin's lips curled. 'You always look so correctly professional, Maitland.'

I closed the report-book with a snap and sat back in my chair. 'Don't you, when you are on duty?'

Her eyelashes were very black and long. Her eyes, in the strip-lighting, were more brilliant than any jewels I had ever seen.

'My dear,' she said, as she drifted into a chair, 'I really must hand it to you! You can keep up a pose better than anyone I have ever met.' Then her voice and expression sharpened. 'But you can drop it with me, Clare Maitland. I've seen through it.'

'What do you mean?'

'I mean,' she said in the same tone, 'that I know just how far your ministering-angel-with-a-soft-voice-and-gentle-expression goes. Not skin deep.'

She smiled, but it was not a pleasant smile.

I said, 'I still don't know what you mean.'

'I was at the Rugger dance! I saw what you were like and what you were after! You're clever. You knew Andrew Darvie before anyone else – and you never let on. And all the time everyone was thinking how sweet and good you were to let your beloved Bill go without a struggle. Oh, you put up a wonderful act. And all the time you couldn't care less. You had heard there was something better in line, and you were after it, or rather him.'

I stared at her, as her words sunk in. I was first incredulous, then angry. Could she really mean what she was saying? Possibly? Then, as I realised that she did, something happened inside me, and I did a thing I would never have thought I could do. I roared with laughter.

She was watching me with a curious expression on her lovely face. 'I never thought you had a sense of humour,' she said softly.

'Look.' I stood up. 'What is all this about? Is your engagement to Bill over, and, if so, why have you come to me?'

'My dear, you're the obvious person,' she drawled. 'As I told you, the whole hospital, except me, knows how desolated you were by his falling for me. I know it was the best thing that ever happened to you. It left you free to pursue a far better prospect.'

'Even supposing it did,' I said, 'which I won't even discuss for it's too foolish, what has it to do with you?'

She said, 'I think it may have a great deal to do with both of us. You want what I want. I thought I'd just come and tell you that you can have any man in the hospital you like, but you are not going to have Andrew Darvie.'

She stood up, too, and smiled as she had before. 'If you try it on, I'll just do what I did before. I'll take him away from you, in full view of the whole hospital. It'll be great fun for you, won't it? To have two crashing jilts?'

I had stopped being amused. I was white with anger. But all the time at the back of my mind a thought stayed, heavy as lead. This was the girl Hugh loved. She would break his heart as easily and as thoughtlessly as she did everything else. If I pretended that I was interested in Andrew, it would make her desperate, and then perhaps Hugh might see her as she really was, before it was too late. 'I'm not in love with Bill,' I said.

'You're not in love …' She sounded unbelievably relieved.

'I did not say that.'

Her perfect face was pale, and her eyes deep gentian pools. 'That's going to be your line? You are in love with Andrew?'

'I don't know about "line",' I said coolly. 'But I am in love.'

'Well, I've warned you –' She broke off and I saw her face change. It was extraordinary, as if she had turned a page of pictures, and the picture she now showed in place of that mask of anger was her usual calm, amused self.

'Hello, Hugh.' She smiled over my shoulder.

‘Looking for someone?’

‘Yes.’ Hugh’s immense height filled the doorway behind me. ‘I was wondering where Nurse Evans was?’ He did not look at me, he did not take his eyes off Sheila.

Sheila turned to me casually. ‘Have you hidden her somewhere?’

‘She’s sterilising in the basement.’

Hugh said, still staring at Sheila, ‘I’ve got her pen. She lent it to me this afternoon. I thought she might be needing it.’

‘She’ll be up in a moment. Will you wait, or shall I keep it for her?’ I said.

He glanced down at me. ‘Oh, thanks, Nurse Maitland.’

‘Well,’ said Sheila, ‘I can’t hang around any longer. Thanks for the jolly chat, Maitland,’ she drawled. She smiled up at Hugh through her fantastic lashes, ‘You coming my way, Hugh?’

He smiled back at her in a way I had never seen him smile. He said lightly, almost cheerfully, ‘Why not? Are you free for dinner?’

As they went out he glanced back casually. ‘Good night, Nurse Maitland.’

‘Good night,’ I said.

Sheila said nothing. She went out with him, without even a backward glance.

Next morning the hospital awoke to find itself in the middle of a moderately severe ’flu epidemic. The probationer in Margaret Ward was one of the first. Mr. Hedley and three of the house-surgeons were the van of the medical staff, who all went down with it in twos and threes in the next couple of weeks. Probationers all over the hospital were laid low, as the young nurses often are, being unused to meeting the many infections to which, over the years, you develop an immunity. The sick-nurses' ward, Florence, was overflowing.

By the time the illness hit the more senior members of the nursing staff there were no beds to spare in Florence, and when Sister Theatre was forced to report sick herself five days later, she was warded in her own room in the Sisters' Home.

'I'm very grateful that I can stay here, Nurse Maitland,' she told me when I went across to visit her for a few minutes in the middle of the afternoon. 'It does mean you can drop across if you are worried about anything, without having to brave Sister Florence each time!'

Sister Florence, quite rightly, regarded sick nurses as patients only, and refused to allow them to be bothered by anything concerning work.

When I got back to the Theatre I found Jenny and Hugh engrossed with the log-book. Hugh looked up and nodded coolly. ''Afternoon, Nurse Maitland.' Then he turned his attention back to the book. This was his usual behaviour with me these days. Since the night when he had walked in on Sheila and me, and then walked away with Sheila, he had barely spoken more than a couple of words to me, and what he had said was invariably to do with our work.

Jenny, who for all her light-heartedness had a very strong sense of etiquette, stood back politely.

'Mr. Sanders wanted to check up on a decompression he did last week, Sister. I was just finding the place for him. Will you carry on now?'

Hugh's head jerked up. 'Sister, Nurse Maitland?'

Jenny's eyes danced, but her voice was serious. 'Haven't you noticed that Nurse Maitland is wearing a sister's belt, Mr. Sanders?'

Hugh glanced at my waistline. In our hospital, all acting sisters were lent an official belt by Matron's office. Anyone wearing one of those belts was always addressed as 'Sister'.

'I'm afraid I hadn't,' he said dryly. 'You are doing quite well these days, aren't you, Sister Maitland?' The way his voice accentuated that title made me squirm inwardly.

I said 'Yes.' I was not sure exactly what he meant, but I knew he meant a great deal more than he said. I was certain that he had heard the last part of my conversation with Sheila. I was equally certain that she would have embroidered on that conversation over their dinner-date. He probably now thought as she thought.

She had persuaded Bill; so why could she not persuade Hugh? That she had tried seemed to me obvious. He made no attempt to hide his hostility. Perhaps he, like she, thought I should now fall gladly into Bill's arms, and again, as she had done, decided my only reason for not so doing was that I had hopes of wealthy marriage with Andrew.

I turned away, forgetting I had not answered Jenny. She was looking at me curiously. 'Shall I stay here, then, Sister?'

'I'm sorry,' I apologised. 'I was thinking of something else. Yes, do that, please. I want to check the instrument cupboard.'

'I'll do that,' she said quickly. Checking the instruments was part of the Staff Nurses' routine.

'No, thank you.' I pushed open the swing-doors into the main Theatre and left them alone.

Some minutes later I heard Andrew's cheerful voice. 'Hello, Nurse Evans. Hello, Sanders, I hear you are now carrying the hospital.'

Hugh's quiet voice said, 'Yes,' and Jenny broke in:

'Are you Senior Surgical Officer, Mr. Sanders? As well as running the Head Unit?'

'Sir Inister does that,' said Hugh, 'and, yes, I'm standing in for the rest.'

Andrew said, 'I was going to work out a schedule with Nurse Maitland. Perhaps you would rather do it.'

Hugh said, 'No. You fix it, and let me know the result.'

'Right,' said Andrew. 'Is she about, Nurse Evans?'

I called from the Theatre, 'I'm in here. I'll be with you in a second.'

Hugh said, 'I've finished this, thanks, Nurse Evans. I want to write it up. Mind if I take the book into the Surgeons' Room?'

Jenny called, 'Is that all right, Sister?'

'Quite.' I closed the instrument cupboard and came back to the duty-room. 'We won't need the book.'

He nodded to Jenny and went out, taking no notice of me. I saw Andrew's look of surprise and Jenny's faint shrug. So it was not all my imagination. They saw something was wrong, too.

Andrew sat at the desk beside me and we went through all the cases that would have to be done over the weekend. Then he said, 'By the way, you've had an apology coming to you for the past week, Clare.'

I said, 'Have I?' I guessed what he was going to say.

'I'm sorry I snapped at you that day old Hedley passed out. I knew it wasn't you who was being clumsy!'

'I shouldn't let it worry you. It didn't worry me. Honestly.'

'I'm glad of that.' He half-turned in his chair to look at me. 'I would never want to worry you, Clare.'

He fiddled with a pencil on the desk. 'Did you enjoy yourself in Scotland?'

'Very much. Mrs. MacFallor couldn't have been sweeter; the scenery was perfect, and it never rained more than once a day!'

He did not smile back as I had expected, instead he said, 'I remember you said that in your letters.' Then he added quickly, 'Why did you only write twice?'

I said, 'Because you never wrote more than twice yourself.'

'Did you mind that?'

'I didn't mind,' I said thoughtfully. 'I wondered why not.'

He grinned, the old mischievous grin of his first few weeks in Augustine's. Andrew also had changed since I had been away. He now seemed older and, strangely, harder. 'The reason I did not write again, after the first two weeks, was that your own letters were so unconsciously filled with loneliness and I was so sorry for you, that the last thing I wanted to do was to hurt you. I was afraid, if I wrote, that I might. Do you blame me?'

'But, Andrew –' I was too surprised to be formal – 'how could your letters hurt me?'

He said slowly, 'I've a weakness. I sometimes say more than I feel.'

'You think I might have misconstrued what you said?'

He shrugged. 'Do you recollect anything I said to you before you went away?'

I said, 'I remember one thing. You warned me about frying-pans and fires.'

'Well, that can work in two ways.'

'You were afraid I might fall in love with your letters?' I asked coolly.

He put both hands down flat on the table in front of us and leant forward. 'You? I? Does it matter which way? Or which of us thought we were in love with the other? We were both dead set to do something on a rebound. And one can make an awful lot of mistakes when one's in a hurry for love.'

'Yes,' I said bleakly. I was thinking not, as he thought, of Bill, but of Hugh. And Sheila.

'Cheer up, love,' he said suddenly in his old friendly way. 'Cheer up.' He had been sitting beside me all this time. Now he turned my way quickly, and before I realised what he was doing, he had kissed me lightly on the mouth.

'We're a pair of complete mugs, you and I, dear Nurse – beg pardon, Sister Maitland. As one mug to another, I salute you!'

He had got up and gone before I had time to get my breath. I heard him greet Jenny in the corridor, 'Good supper, Nurse Evans?'

'Fine, thanks,' said Jenny absently, and she came in to me.

'Hello, you just back? Come and sit down and I'll tell you what's been settled,' I said.

'Right,' she said in the same vague tone. Then, as she sat down, she said, 'I got back a few minutes ago. I was nattering to our Mr. Sanders about broken heads.'

'I didn't hear you.' I sorted the papers on the desk.

'I'm not surprised,' she said dryly. 'We couldn't hear you. But the door was half open and we could see.'

'Oh!' I looked at her properly, her eyes were alight with laughter. 'You pulled a fast one on me, dear Sister. I never knew he cared!'

'Jenny, don't be absurd. You know he was only playing.'

'I'm shocked at your playing on duty,' she said

primly, then she grinned. 'I saw it all. I saw you were as shaken as we were.'

'We?'

'I told you, I was talking to Hugh Sanders. And I said to the great Mr. S., "I never knew he cared." And do you know what Mr. S. said?'

'No?' I held my breath as I waited for her answer.

'He said,' she mimicked Hugh's deep, slow voice, "Didn't you, Nurse Evans? It seems that for once your information service is at fault".'

Jenny yawned sleepily as we left the dining-room together at twenty-past seven the next morning. 'I begin to feel my age after a late night these days, Clare.'

'The rot really sets in around twenty-five, and you're just about due to reach that great age! But I did not know you were gallivanting last night? I thought you were going to bed early? How come, with your Mike ill in bed?'

She said her Mike had dragged himself off his sick-bed. 'He said if he stared at the wall another moment he would start crawling up it.'

'Jenny, you didn't let him go out? He had a temp yesterday morning.'

'No. I'm not that daft. There was a minor "do" in the residents' sitting-room. It turned into a major "do" about midnight. I finally crept to bed at one – and aren't I regretting it this morning!'

I looked at her anxiously. 'You aren't getting 'flu?'

She smiled. 'Not me. I'm only plain tired. I've a hangover from coffee. They had nothing but beer, and I can't drink beer.'

We had reached the Theatre. I unlocked the outer door and we waited in the dark corridor for the strip lighting to blaze on.

'Who was there?' I asked.

She said the usual people. 'Several pale convalescent housemen and their girl friends, a pair of revoltingly healthy physicians who told us all to have cold baths and avoid 'flu; our dear friend Sheila, naturally. No hospital party is complete without her.'

'Who was she with?' I asked casually. 'Hugh?'

Jenny's voice was equally casual. 'If I wasn't so sure how you felt about that man, Clare, I would say you had a thing for him.' The light flickered, then flashed steadily, and we blinked in the shadowless brilliance.

'No,' Jenny swung off her cape, 'she was with Andy, of course. Do you want me to do the syringes first?'

'Please. I'll do my usual gloves.' I hung up my own cape.

Jenny brought the large white tray-load of syringes into the duty-room. 'All right if I do these in here?'

'Fine.'

She inspected her first syringe carefully. 'Changing the subject, I don't understand this bee in your bonnet about our Mr. S. and the glamorous Sheila.'

I twirled the glove in my hand almost savagely. 'The whole Theatre had the same idea for months. Sister talked to me about it before I went to Scotland. You and Angie both mentioned it in your letters. And,' I ended more quietly, 'I use my eyes.'

Jenny tested a second syringe before answering. Then she said, 'I'm beginning to think that I don't.'

'What?'

'Use my eyes,' she said gently. She looked across at me with an expression that was both amazed and kind. I lowered my own eyes and examined the glove I was holding, wishing I had not said so much.

'Perhaps you are right,' she went on. 'We all had the same idea. I expect the Rugger dance was in most of our heads. I know that's what gave me the impression he was taken with her – and your friend Angie Shane said the same. Where Sister Theatre got it from, I just can't guess.'

I said, 'I don't have to guess. I know. Sister Margaret Ward.'

Jenny said, 'Who got it from dear Sheila, her own Staff Nurse. Which knocks that "fact" on the head for a start.'

'It doesn't.' I told her what Sister Theatre had said about recognising when a surgeon was in love.

'She doesn't have to be a Sister to see that! I, Jenny Evans, a mere Staff Nurse, saw that.'

I collected up my pile of gloves. 'Well, there you are. I'm going to do the dispensary list.'

I was thoroughly annoyed with myself by now for giving away so much. The only comforting thought was that my secret was safe with Jenny. She might gossip madly about the hospital in general, but she was a perfect clam where her particular friends were concerned. It was as well to have one comfort, I thought bleakly. There was precious little anywhere else. Jenny had said nothing that could disprove the fact that Hugh loved Sheila. And there was so much more to it than she knew. The way he had been unable to take his eyes off her the other evening; the way he now ignored everyone else. No, that wasn't true, I thought quickly. He never ignored Jenny. Only myself.

The telephone-bell interrupted my dispensary ordering and my unpleasant thoughts. It was Sister Casualty.

'You in charge, Nurse Maitland?'

'Yes, Sister.'

'Have you got the steam up in your sterilisers?'

'Not yet, Sister. The list isn't due to start before half-past nine.' It was five past eight then.

'Well, turn it on,' she said briefly. 'Mind you, Nurse, this is just an unofficial warning, but as I knew Sister was sick, I thought I'd let you know at once. I don't doubt you'll hear from the house-surgeon shortly.'

I said, 'Thank you, Sister. What case is it?'

'Road accident. Father and son. Just admitted to Leyton Ward now. Their car telescoped into the back of a lorry.'

'I am sorry. And they're both very bad?'

'The father's bad enough,' she said shortly. 'But it's the lad that bothers me. And it's the lad I imagine will come down to you. A nice-looking child. Eleven.'

I said quietly, 'What's wrong, Sister?'

She told me. 'I don't like the look of that leg,' she finished. 'I don't like the look of it at all.'

Jenny appeared anxiously at my shoulder. 'Steam-up?' she mouthed. I nodded.

'What do you think Mr. Sanders will do, Sister?' I asked.

I heard her sigh. 'I'm afraid there's little he can do.' She sighed again. 'It seems criminal. A child of that age, with all his life ahead.' I shut my eyes suddenly as I saw what she feared. I opened them again and thanked her for letting me know.

'That's all right, Nurse.' I thought she had finished, when she added, 'If people only saw what we see in the Casualty department of any hospital, speed limit or no speed limit, they would never drive at more than thirty miles an hour with a child in the car. Endanger your own life and limb if you must! But not your children! Think how that father will feel if his lad loses his leg. And I don't see how Mr. Sanders or any other surgeon can save it.'

Jenny came back as I replaced the receiver. 'What is it?'

I told her what Sister Casualty had said. 'Sister Cas. never panics, never exaggerates,' I ended.

'I know.' Jenny looked at me and I looked at her. She seemed years older now than the girl I had been talking to half an hour ago. I don't know if I looked it, but I felt the same. Ages older.

I pulled myself together. 'Will you set it? I'll organise the pros, then I'll take it and you "dirty". I don't think it would be fair to make the girls do much. They're too young.'

'Right.'

I reached up and switched on the red warning-light over the Theatre.

When that light was on the Theatre was out of bounds to anyone not wearing a mask and gown.

Five minutes later the telephone rang again. It was Andrew. 'How soon can you have the Theatre ready, Nurse Maitland?'

I glanced at the clock. 'Fifteen minutes from now.'

'Thank Heaven for that. But I thought you needed twenty at least to get up the steam?'

I told him that Sister Casualty had warned us.

'Thank Heaven for that,' he said again. 'And turn the heat up. This poor child is pretty shocked.'

'His right leg, isn't it?'

'Yes.'

'What is Mr. Sanders going to do?' I prayed that the answer might not be the one I expected.

Andrew said slowly, 'I'm afraid he's got little option. I've never seen anything so bad myself.'

'What does Mr. Sanders say?' I heard someone

come into the duty-room as I spoke. I turned and saw Hugh behind me. He nodded, as Andrew's voice went on, 'He hasn't said anything. Just that he wants the boy in the Theatre at once.' Andrew was silent for a second, then he said, 'Clare, think of it. A child of that age. All through a bit of carelessness.'

I said, 'Yes.'

His voice changed again. 'I'll tell the ward, eight-twenty-five. That right?'

'Quite right. Thank you.'

I put down the receiver and turned to Hugh. He jerked his head at the telephone. 'Darvie?'

'Yes, Mr. Sanders.'

'In a quarter of an hour? Can you manage that?'

'Yes, Mr. Sanders.' I thought I had never seen any man look so worried.

'You'll be taking the case for me?'

Again I said 'Yes.' He was silent and I hated to bother him, but I had to know exactly what he would be needing. I said:

'Mr. Darvie seems to think there's not much you can do. Is there anything special you'd like in the way of instruments?'

His mouth was a straight line, a small muscle twitched high in his cheek. 'You had better have all the usual ready – in case I can't save it for him.'

'Do you think you can? Possibly?'

I saw him wince at his own thoughts. Then he said, 'I've just had a talk with the father. I didn't like to do it, but he is the next-of-kin, and although he's pretty knocked about, he's not too bad himself. He was overtaking, and the boy got the brunt of it. The lorry was on the inside. I had to tell him what might have to be done.'

'What did he say?'

He looked down at me steadily. 'He said what they all say, "I leave it to you, doctor. I know you'll do what's best".'

I waited for him to go on, but he said nothing. I was anxious about the time. I was not yet changed, and I was worried about things in the Theatre. I knew Jenny was completely reliable, but I was in charge and I wanted to be in there seeing things for myself. Hospital etiquette and common humanity both ruled that I should stay where I was, waiting for this desperately worried young man to decide what he was going to have to do. I glanced unconsciously at the clock over the door. Hugh noticed this.

'I won't keep you any longer,' he said formally. 'I'll go and change now.' But still he did not move. Then he said suddenly, 'How can I do it, Clare? How can I? A boy of that age. How can I?'

The words seemed to force their way out of his mouth; his hands were thrust deep into his pockets in his usual attitude; but his normally straight shoulders were hunched wearily, as if the weight of the appalling responsibility he carried was too great, even for him. He alone was qualified to make and would have to make the decision. Everyone else connected with this boy, in the ward and the Theatre, would follow. Hugh would have to lead alone.

'Hugh,' I said quietly, using his Christian name intentionally, although I knew mine had slipped out, 'you can only do as that father said.' His gaze flickered, then stayed on my face, as if I were a stranger talking. 'Not even the best surgeon in England can work a miracle. And you must know we all consider you the best surgeon in the hospital. We know that whatever you do will be the only possible thing.'

'You all think that?' He sounded incredulous.

'We do,' I said firmly.

He nodded and moved to the door. He said politely, 'Thank you for what you've just said.'

I knew he thought I had only spoken to comfort him, that it was something I had dreamed up on the spur of the moment.

'One moment, Mr. Sanders.' I slipped back into formality, unconsciously. 'I meant what I said. If this child were my brother or my son I would still rather have you in charge of the case than any other surgeon I know.'

He did not answer, he merely inclined his head slowly. It was more than a nod, less than a bow. Then he walked heavily away to the Surgeons' room …

Sister Leyton Ward herself came down to the Theatre with the small boy. Hugh and Andrew were scrubbing at the sinks when we heard the faint rumble of the rubber-wheeled trolley-stretcher. Hugh, his shirt-sleeves rolled high, his black hair hidden beneath a cap, his face masked, looked over his shoulder.

Andrew's eyes were troubled. 'I said we'd have to patch him up a bit. I thought he was too shocked to take anything more.'

Hugh said grimly, 'So he is, but that's nothing to how shocked he'll be if he has to wake up without his leg.'

'Would you like me to have a word with him now?' asked Andrew uncertainly.

Hugh was already across the Theatre. 'I'll do it. The onus is on me.' The door closed soundlessly behind him.

Andrew rinsed, soaped, scrubbed his hands, rinsed again. 'Rather him than me,' he murmured.

Hugh came back in a few minutes. We all looked at him, but not one of us dared ask what had happened.

The gallery filled up the way it always did fill, even at this early hour, when there was something unusual happening in the Theatre. No one ever knew how the students heard about emergencies. There was no briefing, no enforced attention, no time in a crisis to let anyone not directly concerned know what we were doing; but the students heard somehow and came. I looked up once and saw without surprise that all the seats were taken.

Then I forgot about the gallery. I forgot about everything but the boy on the table and the row of silver in front of me, and, above all, the brown-gloved hands that moved from my trolley to that boy, back and forward, safe and sure, back and forward.

Sister Leyton stood beside me and Jenny hovered, silent, efficient, there when she was needed, out of the way when not.

The anaesthetist looked up. 'Any hope?' he added quietly.

Hugh said, quite calmly, 'I'm not certain yet what I can do. But I know what I am not going to do. I'm not going to cripple this boy for life. I'm going all out for the alternative.' He glanced at the anaesthetist. 'How's he taking things your end?'

'All right here,' said the anaesthetist.

Hugh turned to me formally. 'I won't want any of those things, Sister. Can you get me the alternative set, please?'

Jenny was already pushing forward the spare trolley we had set, almost hopelessly, but just in case. 'The other trolley is ready now, Mr. Sanders,' I said.

The students in the gallery craned forward. It isn't

every day one gets a front row seat at a miracle.

Hugh's steady, patient, clever fingers worked on. Andrew followed him carefully. The anaesthetist checked. I threaded needles, handed instruments, swabs, over and over again, replacing the instruments each time in their right order on my trolley. That order is important. Few surgeons turn to look for what they want; they reach a hand behind them and pick up the right thing, almost by instinct.

I lost all count of time. It seemed hours later that Hugh said, 'Nurse Evans, please will you release the tourniquet slowly.' Jenny did as he said, and everyone watching waited, and held their breath.

Hugh said, 'Thank you.' He straightened his back, lifted his hands, and stood away from the table. Andrew did the same. The anaesthetist jerked his head up sharply, and he, too, waited.

Then, only a few seconds, minutes, or years, passed, before Hugh said, 'Feel his foot, please, Nurse.'

Jenny did as she was told.

'How is it?'

No one moved on the floor or in the gallery. Then we heard Jenny's clear voice, 'Warm, Mr. Sanders.' Her voice choked, then she controlled it. 'Quite warm,' she repeated.

And a sigh went round the Theatre. A sigh, as gentle and as comforting as a summer breeze on a thunder-heavy day.

Hugh's voice was colourless, 'Thank you, Nurse Evans.' He nodded at Andrew and said what all surgeons say at the end of a successful case, 'All right. That's it.' Over his shoulder to me he added, 'I'll want to put this in plaster afterwards, Sister.'

I said, 'We have it ready, Mr. Sanders.'

It was another hour before the Theatre was clear and we were able to relax for a few minutes. It was only a question of minutes, because the work scheduled for that morning had still to be done in the annexe.

'Will they have lunch first, or go straight on?' asked Jenny quietly.

'I'll find out. If they decide to go on, I'll take the list, and Martin can "dirty" for me. You and Smith nip off to lunch.'

I knocked on the Surgeons' room door. The three men were drinking tea.

Hugh pushed his hand through his thick black hair. 'What have we to do?' He frowned at his own forgetfulness, then remembered. 'Three appendices and two repairs.' He glanced at the clock. 'Nearly twelve. We might as well carry straight on. That suit you, Sister?'

'Of course. Then I'll ring the wards.'

Andrew stood up. 'I can do that for you. I expect you're pretty busy.'

'Thank you,' I said gratefully. Hugh said no more, so I left them to their tea. I was out in the corridor again before I discovered that Hugh had followed me. He said, 'Thank you very much for your help just now.'

'I didn't do anything,' I said honestly. 'But you –' I couldn't go on. I was afraid of what I might say.

He said simply, 'You helped me. Thank you,' and went back into the Surgeons' room.

Jenny came to relieve me for my lunch at one. Matron sent us a spare probationer, so I collected Nurse Martin and took her with me. 'And don't come back from lunch, Nurse. You go off-duty.'

'Oh, no, Sister, please. Not when we're so busy. I can't.'

'You certainly can, my child,' I said, 'or I really will behave like a Sister. Of course you girls must have your time off. You can't work from seven-thirty to nine.'

She smiled. 'But you and Nurse Evans are doing so.'

'That's a Staff Nurse's privilege,' I said firmly. 'And when you're a Staff Nurse you can stay on duty, too. Won't that be nice for you?' She laughed and rushed away.

At three the annexe was clear again. The men left for their belated lunch, while Jenny, the two pros and I cleaned, scrubbed, washed and boiled every movable thing in the Theatre and the annexe. At half-past four an emergency appendix was admitted for immediate operation, and at ten minutes to six a seaman, who had been in a fight, had a plaster of Paris splint put on his broken wrist in our annexe.

'One thing about hospital life is that there's never a dull moment,' said Jenny as she mopped the plaster-stained annexe floor. 'One may be harassed, one may even wear one's fingers to the bone, but one is never bored. No, indeed.'

'Sister,' said Nurse Martin, 'do you suppose we'll have anything else today?'

I balanced with my chin the pile of plaster-bandage tins I was carrying. 'I wouldn't like to say. It's only seven-thirty now. Certainly, I've just seen Sister Casualty in Matron's office, and she says Casualty is clear. But what goes for one moment of the day doesn't go for the next.'

But Sister Casualty was right. No more emergencies came in for the rest of the evening, and the day finished quietly. I went to late supper, and when I returned at half-past eight I sent a protesting Jenny off for the first time that day.

'I hate leaving you,' she said.

'My dear, don't be absurd. There's only another half-hour. What can happen in half an hour?'

'Asking for it,' she complained to the ceiling. 'If ever a girl asked for it!'

I laughed. 'Well, I'm on call tonight, anyway. It'll save me coming across! But, seriously, do go. I promise I'll ring the Home at once if there's a crisis. And for goodness' sake see that those girls get off in time for Chapel. Home Sister will be furious if they are late. She always takes Chapel herself on Saturday nights.'

'Is it really still Saturday?' Jenny rubbed her eyes.

'Well, off you go. And take my hint, and don't gallivant. Tell your Mike to stay in bed and be grateful he's there.'

She smiled. 'I can't see any of our poor wretched surgeons having enough energy for a party tonight. I doubt if even dear Sheila could galvanize them to life tonight. What a day!'

When they had all gone, I walked round the rooms, seeing that they were tidy and ready for any sudden case. I turned off lights and closed doors, leaving the darkness behind me. As I went round I thought about Sheila and the other side of my life. It seemed a long way away. It seemed almost unimportant.

It would be easy to become totally absorbed in any hospital. There was so much to do, so much to give. Wasn't that enough for anyone? I stood still in the corridor, thinking this over.

Would it be enough for me? I loved my job, but would it be enough?

I thought suddenly, 'Would I love it so much if

there were no Hugh? Would I love it more?'

A pain, such as I had never felt, took hold of me. From the time I had discovered I loved him, that day when he left me in Scotland, I had hoped. It had not been clear what I was hoping. Not that he would love me, that would be asking too much from life, but that he would always be around the hospital for me to love.

My professional self noticed that a light had been left on in the Surgeons' room. I opened the door and reached my hand round to switch it off, when I saw someone was sitting at the small table. A sheaf of notes was spread on the table-top, and the man's head was resting on his arms. I recognised Hugh's black hair.

I stood watching him for a few seconds, then I said quietly, 'Mr. Sanders.'

He raised his head slowly, opened his eyes, and smiled at me. It was a wonderful smile. He said simply, 'I was dreaming about you, Clare.' He shook his head slightly and stood up. 'I'm sorry to clutter up your Theatre,' he said. 'I must be growing old. I've never fallen asleep like that before.'

I was still too shaken by his first words to think straight.

'It's not old age,' I said seriously. 'It's strain.'

He smiled faintly. 'You had me worried. I didn't exactly consider that at thirty-two I should have one foot in the grave.'

I said, 'I – we all thought you were wonderful this morning.'

'You mean you thought my surgery was all right this morning,' he corrected me gently. 'Do you know what finally made me take that chance?'

'It wasn't as bad as you had expected?'

‘It was every bit as bad,’ he said soberly. ‘No. You remember when I went out to talk to him?’

‘Yes.’

‘I said, “Look, old chap, I may not be able to mend that leg.” He looked up at me with great round eyes and grinned. Clare, he actually laughed. “You mean I’ll be like Long John Silver?” I said, “That’s right.” He kept on grinning. “Expect they’ll call me Long John Adam at school, doctor,” was all he said.’ Hugh’s mouth closed in a straight line as I had seen this morning. ‘So I thought that if he could help me that much, I could go ahead,’ he said quietly.

‘When will you know if he’s out of the wood?’

He shook his head. ‘In a few days. It’ll mean just waiting, hanging around, waiting.’ He sighed. ‘I seem to spend my life doing that these days … Waiting.’

I said ‘Yes.’ I was thinking of Sheila. She might have been in the room with us, I felt her presence so strongly.

He tucked his notes under his arm and opened the door for me. He glanced up the empty corridor. ‘You all alone?’

‘Yes. The calm after the storm. All that now remains is for me to fill in the day’s log in the report-book.’

He said, ‘Do you want any help? After all,’ he smiled, I was there, too.’

‘I’d be very grateful if you would,’ I said. ‘I can remember what was used and on whom, but it does take an effort. My brain feels addled tonight.’

‘You’re not getting ’flu?’

‘I must be tired,’ I thought, ‘to imagine he really sounded concerned. ‘Not me.’ I led the way in to the duty-room. I expected him to take Sister’s chair at the desk, but he left that for me, and carried one forward from its place against the wall.

'Where's the report-book?' he asked, seating himself beside me. 'Now, what do you want to know?' He glanced over my shoulder as he spoke, then, reading the headings in the book, he dictated the report. I wrote steadily for ten minutes, and then it was finished.

He sat in his chair, looked at me for a few seconds, then he said, 'You've never quite got over your dislike of me, have you, Clare? Oh, I know you've been very polite, very kind about my work,' he went on quickly. 'But myself, as a person, you can't tolerate.'

'I can't?' I was too surprised to say anything else.

'My dear girl, you don't have to pretend. Surely, what with one thing and another, we know each other well enough to talk openly. I was going to ask … Oh it's not really important. I'm sure you must be very tired.'

'I'm exhausted,' I said.

The muscle I had seen this morning was now working again, high in his cheek. I stared at it, as if it could explain his strange behaviour.

'Well, I was going to ask you –'

'Yes?'

'If you are seriously thinking of marrying Andrew Darvie?'

I had expected a good many questions, but not that one. All I said was 'Why?'

'I should be interested in your answer,' he said calmly.

'People are always asking me questions these days,' I said bitterly. 'Ever since Bill dropped me I've been cross-examined by everyone I know.' I said the words on purpose. 'And when I want to know something myself, no one tells me anything.'

'Poor Clare.' His voice softened suddenly. 'What do you want to know?'

'Why do you care if I'm going to marry Andrew?'

'That wasn't what I said,' he said dryly, and his face wore the old remote look. He was Mr. Sanders again, and we were back in the Theatre. For a few minutes today we had broken away from that, we had come near to our friendly, pleasant relationship in Scotland. But not now. Again we had regressed.

'I take it, by your silence, that you are thinking of marrying him,' he said. 'I must congratulate you. Darvie should make you a most suitable husband.' His lips twisted on the word 'suitable'.

I sat back and dropped my hands in my lap. Whatever he thought of me, I loved him, and I could not let him go on thinking that.

'I'm not going to marry Andrew Darvie, Bill Blake, or anyone else,' I said flatly. 'No one's asked me to marry them. I'm single, unattached, unwanted. That's all there is to it. If your Sheila has told you anything else, she's wrong. I know I led her up the garden-path about Andrew. I did it on purpose. I know I shouldn't have done it, but I did. I'm sorry now. I wasn't sorry then. And you can tell her – oh, you can tell her what you like! Goodnight!'

I could not get up and make a fine exit, my legs would not have carried me if I had. I sat where I was and closed my eyes. When I opened them again, I thought I would be alone.

I heard him move, and I sighed with something like relief. It would be better when he was gone. I opened my eyes to find he was still there, leaning against the closed Theatre door, watching me. He was looking at me, as I have never seen any man look at me before, and the expression in his eyes made my heart turn over.

He said, 'Do you mind my still being here?'

'No.'

Then he said quietly, 'Why did you call her "my" Sheila?'

'Isn't she?'

He shook his head. 'Why do you think I asked her out the other night?'

'Because you wanted to.'

He shook his head again and dug his hands in his pockets. 'As you've been so honest, my darling, I feel a little honesty is due from me. I asked her because I was so angry that I had to do something.'

'Why were you angry?'

'I had just heard you say you were in love with Darvie.'

I rubbed my forehead. 'But that was only one evening. You've been in love with her for months. The whole hospital knows that.'

'The hospital can know what it likes,' he said calmly. 'I've certainly been in love for months – since the day you got back from your holiday to be accurate – but not with Sheila Mandin.'

I said, 'But you can't have been in love with me? Not when you've seen her.'

He said gently, 'My poor darling, you really mean that, don't you? I wish you hadn't been so hurt. You mustn't think that way. No man who loved you could love her. You aren't the same type. You've nothing in common.'

I said, 'Why did you behave the way you did? All this time?'

He smiled. 'How else could I behave? I met you. I thought, "That's it", and what did I find? That you were engaged to one of my best friends. So I pushed off, and saw you at the Rugger dance with Darvie. And because I wanted you to smile at me the way you smiled at Darvie, I dared to criticise, apparently, on Bill's behalf. I then find I've put my foot in it all round, and, not surprisingly, you can't bear the sight of me. I came up to Scotland to see you. I hoped I might have more of a chance up there. You know what happened then.'

'But I came back?'

He shook his head. 'Indeed you came back, and I hung around this Theatre all day, only to hear you telling Sheila Mandin that you were in love with someone else – and a few nights later I see you, here, being kissed by Darvie.' He sighed. 'I haven't talked so much for years. But I wanted you to know, Clare.'

It was all so wonderful that I could not believe any of it. I said the first thing that came into my head. 'What are you doing standing over there against the wall?'

He moved away and came slowly towards me. He towered over the table. 'When you closed your eyes just now I wanted, more than anything else in the world, to hold you in my arms.' His eyes were very gentle. 'Would you have minded?'

I looked up at him. I said, 'No.'

He stood quite still. His face looked as if a light had been turned on inside him. He said, 'You don't dislike me?'

'No.'

He said, very quietly, 'I have not forgotten how it felt to hold you in my arms.'

I said, 'I haven't forgotten either, Hugh.'

'You haven't?' He glanced quickly up at the clock and laughed helplessly. 'When are you off-duty, Clare?

If it isn't soon, I'll have to kiss you here and now.'

I said meekly, 'You are the Senior Surgical Officer, Mr. Sanders.'

His hands came across the desk and on to my shoulders as the telephone bell rang between us.

'Theatre. Nurse Maitland speaking.'

It was Sister Casualty again. 'I think I've another appendix for you, Nurse. The porter's just gone up to fetch Mr. Sanders.'

'Mr. Sanders is here, Sister,' I said. 'I'll get him for you.' Hugh held out his hand in mock resignation. I handed him the receiver, then went into the Theatre to turn on the heat.

I heard him say, 'I'll be along in a minute, Sister. Thank you.'

He came in to the Theatre. 'Who's on call? You?'

I looked across the Theatre at him and nodded happily. 'Me. I'm sorry. I'm not off-duty after all.'

He put both his hands in his pockets and smiled at me. 'I didn't know a man could be so happy,' he said simply.

'I did not know I could be either.'

'I'm sorry about this case,' he said. 'It's been a long day for you. Too long. I must get off and see him.'

'Yes.' I could not move either. I was too thunderstruck with happiness to do anything. 'It's been an awful day for you, Hugh.'

He said, 'It's been the best day of my life. But I really must go now. I'll be back.'

As he turned to go, he stopped.

'Clare. There's something we haven't settled.'

'What's that?'

'I haven't asked you to marry me. Will you? Please?'

He stood as I had seen him so many times, with his long white coat flapping round his legs, his stethoscope tucked into his breast pocket, his hands deep in the others. His shoulders were back and his face serious, the way he always stood in the Theatre, when he was anxiously awaiting the result of something.

I said, 'I should love to.'

His face relaxed and he smiled. 'Bless you,' he said, and his voice was deeper than I had ever heard it.

The outer door closed after him. I shot round the Theatre, warmed blankets, checked on the emergency setting, then went to change. I would not call Jenny back to 'dirty' for me, until I was absolutely definite about the case.

Hugh rang me from Casualty a few minutes later. 'Nurse Maitland?' He would be ringing from the porter's lodge, within full hearing of Sam and possibly Sister Casualty.

'Yes, Mr. Sanders?'

'Can you have the Theatre ready by nine-thirty?'

'Yes, Mr. Sanders. Straightforward appendix?'

'Yes. And I say, Nurse Maitland –'

'Yes?'

'I'm so glad to hear of your future plans,' he said smoothly.

When Jenny arrived the Theatre was all ready. The case was a straightforward one as Hugh had foreseen. The patient was back in the wards by ten.

'Leave me the clearing-up, Jenny,' I said. 'It's supposed to be your night off.'

'I wouldn't dream of it.'

'I mean it,' I said. 'I'm not at all tired.'

She pulled her mask off her face. 'You're not? You must be! My feet are falling off.'

'Well, you go after them,' I said. 'At once. Am I or am I not acting-unpaid-Sister Theatre?'

'If you're sure, Clare?' she said uncertainly.

'Run along, my child.'

It did not take me long to clear, clean and re-set the place again. My hands and feet were busy, but my mind for the first time in my nursing career, now that I was alone, refused to concentrate on the job in hand. I had to break through my bubble of happiness and force myself to pay proper attention to what I was doing. When I had finished, I went round thoroughly and saw that I had done everything properly.

I did not know where Hugh was. He was probably going round the wards. He would have a great deal to do. Every surgical case in this thousand-bedded hospital was under his direct care. His day was not over yet.

I turned off all the lights, then stood in the darkness, thinking of him, of how wonderful he was, how wonderful it was all going to be. I could not believe it had all happened. Happiness was going to take getting used to, I thought, as I locked the outer door.

I heard someone coming up the corridor. 'Nurse Maitland, don't lock up for a moment!'

Hugh and Andrew were walking quickly towards me. I put the key back in the lock. 'Another case?' I asked with a smile.

Hugh said calmly, 'No, I've left something behind with you.'

Andrew said, 'I'm always leaving my watch in there.'

'You are?' Hugh nodded. 'Don't wait for me if you're in a hurry.'

'Sure you don't mind? I want to get up to Robert to look at that last chap. I haven't written up his drugs yet.'

'You get on,' said Hugh. 'I'll see you in Leyton in

ten minutes.'

'Right. Good night, Nurse Maitland.'

'Good night, Mr. Darvie.' I had opened the door and switched on the strip lighting.

'What did you leave behind?' I asked Hugh as we waited for the light. 'Stethoscope – pen?'

'Neither.' The light came on and I saw his eyes were dancing. 'I have ten minutes to myself, and after that I belong to the hospital again.' He was leaning against the outer door. 'But I was telling the truth.

'I did leave something here. With you.' He held out his hands. 'You have everything that I possess, Clare. My heart, my love, my life.' And then he kissed me.

In a little while he had to go back to the wards, to the small boy whose leg he had saved, to the pathetically grateful, worried father, to the countless patients who needed him – who would always need him.

As I walked back to the Nurses' Home alone I thought of our life together, and I knew I would often be alone, and waiting for him to be free to come to me. But I knew this was unimportant. We might often have to be apart, because of his work. But neither Hugh nor I would ever be alone again.

# BONUS PREVIEW CHAPTER

# THE GOLDEN HOUR
by Lucilla Andrews

## CHAPTER ONE

The ward seemed four miles long and to contain four hundred beds. All the beds were filled with pale, delicate-looking women who watched me with kind, curious eyes. They must have been watching the other nurses also, but on my first afternoon in Victoria Ward I was convinced that they were all staring at me.

Christine Blake, the other new junior, whispered, 'Alice, I'm scared. They all look so ill.'

The Staff Nurse glanced round coldly. 'Nurse Blake, you will please not chatter while waiting for tea to be served.' She turned to me. 'Nurse Shane, will you take this tray to Mrs. Evans in No. 24? She has acute rheumatism, so she must not feed herself.'

'Yes, Nurse.' I tried to sound efficient but my hands were shaking and when she let go of the neat tray, I knocked the egg from its cup.

'Nurse, that's soft boiled,' she announced unnecessarily, since the shell had broken and the yoke was all over the white tray-cloth. Then she sighed. 'Boil another egg, lay a clean tray, put that cloth to soak, and hurry up about it!'

Having dealt with me, she sent Christine scuttling into the ward with the bread-and-butter, then handed over to the Senior Probationer. 'Carry on for me, Nurse Astor. And don't forget that the diabetics are to eat an hour later because the times of their injections have been altered.'

Nurse Astor was a cool, neat and, to Chris and me, frighteningly efficient young woman of twenty-one. She nodded calmly. 'No, Nurse. Thank you, Nurse.'

When the Staff Nurse had left the kitchen, Nurse Astor smiled at me. 'Don't panic about your egg,' she murmured. 'Everyone expects you to drop things in your first week.'

I stared at her incredulously. 'Did you drop anything, Nurse?'

Her smile broadened. 'Only a bowl of washing water all over Sister Luke. I was working in Luke Ward, and I slipped as I passed her table. She was drenched.'

'Whatever happened?'

'Sister Luke roared with laughter. But then,' she added thoughtfully, 'I must be fair and say that Sister Luke is a perfect sweetie. All the same, not even Sister Victoria will get tough with you in your first week – or month, come to that. It's only after that that they expect you to get a grip on things.'

She had re-filled the tea urn and pushed the trolley out of the kitchen to replenish the teacups in the ward. She looked so capable and I wondered desperately if I would ever reach her state of mind. I had spent weeks in the classrooms in the Preliminary Training School and one day in a ward. Like Chris, I was very scared. And Mrs. Evans, the friendly woman who lay in Bed 24, guessed this at once.

'You won't hurt me, love,' she said encouragingly,

as I slipped a hand under her pillow to raise her head. 'I don't get any pain now. Always lets the new nurses feed me, Sister does. I'm ever such good experience for you, see.'

From my place beside her I managed to count the rows of beds. I was very surprised to find there were only forty beds in Victoria. I had been sure there were so many more. But forty, I discovered, as I raced up and down the ward in the next few days, was more than enough. Chris and I were well-accustomed to being told to hurry up, bustle to, nip along, and anything else that implied moving at the double. We did our best to oblige, not realising that you need to spend over six months in the wards before you can work comfortably at the necessary speed. Occasionally, we were over-zealous and were scolded by Sister for running.

'A nurse may only run in a case of haemorrhage or fire, Nurses!' But according to the Staff Nurse we were not sufficiently zealous with our cleaning. 'Nurse Shane, I can see dust on one of your bed-tables. And that lampshade has a speck of soot on it.'

'Nurse Blake, there is grime on the backs of your lockers.'

'And who,' said Chris bitterly to me later, 'but a Mike's Staff Nurse would go round running her finger along the backs of lockers in London? Of course there was grime. What else can she expect when we are so close to the docks?'

Our hospital was called St. Michael's, and it stood in the East End of London. We loved the proximity to the docks, the sound of the ships' sirens, the faint smell of tar, smoke and salt that was always in the air. But the air was also full of soot.

The soot landed on our lockers and bed-tables and

speckled the white quilts on the patients' beds and caused the Staff Nurse to frown on us several times a day. Chris and I began to despair of ever becoming nurses and felt certain that we would be dismissed from the hospital under a cloud of soot.

At the end of that first week I had my first mid-morning on-duty alone.

In Victoria Ward all the first-year probationers were off from ten until one each day, with the exception of the nurse who was having a day off on the following day. Before Nurse Astor went off-duty that morning she drew me into the kitchen.

'Now you'll be all right, Shane,' she assured me comfortingly. 'I've made you a work-list. Don't lose it. It's quite simple; first, ten o'clock temperatures, then the elevenses – only get them cleared away by eleven. Any odd errands Sister will give you. The doctors finish their rounds by a quarter to twelve and you close the doors, and then wheel in the lunch-trolley as twelve strikes. Remember, while it is actually striking. Sister creates if you are too early or too late. Got that?'

I was nodding like a mandarin. 'Yes, Nurse.'

'And if you get stuck, ask Elsie. She knows the ropes.'

'Aye,' said Elsie, the ward-maid, who had been listening grimly. 'I'll sort her.'

I was almost as frightened of Elsie as I was of Sister. Elsie had ruled the Victoria kitchen for sixteen years and her word was law.

'Thank you, Elsie,' I murmured. Nurse Astor gave me a maternally anxious smile and left us alone.

'Get along, Nurse,' said Elsie. 'I want my kitchen to myself while I heat the milk.'

I went into the ward to take the temperatures. The ward was full of young men and women. St. Michael's was a teaching hospital and there were several hundred students in the medical school. There also seemed to be as many doctors on the hospital staff, although that was hardly possible. Victoria, that morning, was crammed with men and women in long white coats, short white coats, a couple in black professional jackets and pin-striped trousers that even I recognised as Consultants, and rows of students.

Despite the crowd, the ward was very quiet. One Consultant physician was teaching on rheumatism at the far end of the ward. He must have been the senior, because Sister was with him, and the Staff Nurse with the physician teaching on hearts by the door. I did not know their names, but I did not know any doctor's name in Mike's yet and could barely recognise even the faces of the house-men and medical registrars attached to Victoria, a medical ward. The only fact I had grasped, imprinted on me by the helpful Nurse Astor, was that long white coats were registrars and quite important. But one long white coat was the Senior Medical Officer and he was very important so you had to be careful with long white coats. The short coats, Nurse Astor said, were housemen and need not be taken too seriously; and the students counted as little in the hospital hierarchy, she assured me, as did junior nurses.

'Of course, if you ever come face to face with a black professional jacket, Shane, run like a stag for the nearest Sister. That's what Consultants wear.'

I had finished the temperatures and pushed in the rubber-wheeled milk-trolley. Sister caught my eye and I went up to her. 'You are making too much noise, Nurse,' she whispered. 'And you are being too slow. Those drinks should be out of the ward by eleven.'

I said, 'Yes, Sister. I'm sorry, Sister.'

She nodded. 'Directly you have them cleared, I want you to go to the pathological laboratory. Ask for a cilliated tube and bring it straight to me.'

She turned back to her round. I squeezed through the crowd round that particular bed and scampered down the ward collecting cups. The women smiled at me and whispered encouragingly, 'Don't you fret, ducks. You're doing all right. In good time. Honest.'

Chris and I had found our patients a revelation. We had expected them to be ill, which they were, but demanding and impatient, which they were not. And we had not expected their continuous co-operation and encouragement.

'In fact,' as Chris said, 'they look after us, bless 'em, instead of us looking after them!'

I was thinking of this as I picked up the last cup and saw that the woman by whose bed Sister had been standing when she spoke to me was beckoning to me.

'Sister may want that tube for Mrs. Levine, love. The lady in 32. You'd best nip off before Dr. Thatcher gets to her.'

'Thanks,' I whispered breathlessly. 'I will.'

I had never been alone to the Path Lab before, but I knew where it was because while we were in the training school, Sister P.T.S. had taken us on three conducted tours of the hospital. St. Michael's held over a thousand beds and dealt with many thousands of out-patients weekly. Sister P.T.S. had told us that the pathological department was one of the largest and considered one of the best in London. I remembered this now, as I pushed open, rather hesitantly, the door that was cordially labelled, '*Do not bother to knock. Please walk in*'.

I went in. I expected to find a row of clever, bespectacled, youngish men, peering down microscopes and absent-mindedly eating dusty sandwiches, while discovering some rare diseases or blood-group. Instead the large airy room was empty. At the end of the room were four doors, three closed and labelled with various pathologists' names. The fourth stood open and apparently was as empty as the one in which I stood.

I gazed round helplessly at the many microscopes on the zinc-covered tables; the shining white slabs by the sinks; the rows and rows of coloured stone bottles and clean test-tubes on the shelves that lined the walls. I thought of Sister Victoria and of Mrs. Levine in Bed 32. Had Dr. Thatcher reached her yet? Was the whole teaching round waiting impatiently for me and that tube? I began to panic. I would have liked to have helped myself to a tube, but I did not know where the cilliated tubes were kept or even what one looked like. But still less did I like to think of Sister Victoria.

I glanced round and saw a nurse standing behind me.

'Please, Nurse –' I turned thankfully, then realised I was talking to my own reflection in a mirror hanging on the far wall. The morning light fell palely on the glass, and I smiled sheepishly at myself. It was summer, but the gold was missing from the sun and the flat light darkened the faint auburn of my hair to a dull brown. I looked with displeasure at my ruffled cap that was slipping on to the back of my head and never would perch delicately as did Nurse Astor's. I took out the pins and fixed it forward. That was better. But it still looked pinned on and not as if it were floating, which was the angle we all aimed at with our caps.

‘Of course we are quite content to have our department used by nurses who wish to straighten their caps,’ said a quiet voice behind me. ‘But would you be requiring anything else, Nurse? Or would you rather I left you to your hairdressing?’

I spun round, scarlet with embarrassment, then relaxed a little when I saw that the man who had come out of the room I thought empty was dressed in the ubiquitous sports jacket worn by a student. ‘Oh, please,’ I said, ‘can I have a cilliated tube for Victoria Ward?’

He had been wearing horn-rimmed glasses that made him seem older than the usual student. He took them off and rubbed his eyes before answering. ‘A cilliated tube, did you say, Nurse?’ he asked pleasantly.

‘Yes, please.’

He put his glasses in a pocket of his coat without troubling to find the case. ‘For Victoria?’

I nodded and glanced at the clock on the wall. There was a clock on the wall in every department in St. Michael’s, and under those clocks at most hours of the day there was a junior nurse transfixed with horror at the speed with which the hands were racing round. It was already ten minutes since I had left Victoria.

He said, ‘Would you mind saying that again? I think I must have missed something.’

I repeated my request. ‘May I have one now, please?’

He put his hands in his pockets and hunched his shoulders slightly. ‘I’m sorry, but I’m afraid –’ he hesitated – ‘that you cannot.’

‘Please,’ I was quite desperate, ‘I must have one.’ I stared wildly round at the thousands of empty test tubes. ‘Sister Victoria wants one for Dr. Thatcher and he's going round now.'

He broke in, 'For Mrs. Levine?'

I sighed with relief. 'Yes, that's right. Do you know about her? Are you one of the clerks?' A clerk is a student attached to a medical ward.

He looked down at me for a few seconds in silence. He was a very tall young man, and his shoulders, even when hunched as now, were the broadest I had yet seen among his athletic Rugger-playing colleagues in the medical school. His hair was light brown and either very thick or slightly untidy, I was too harassed to bother which. He had a long face with a good brow and a strong jawline. I was in a fever of impatience but since apparently I could not hurry him I considered his appearance. It was preferable to considering Sister Victoria.

Eventually he murmured, 'Yes, I know Mrs. Levine.' He walked leisurely across the room, took two tubes from a shelf and handed them to me.

'Thank you, but I only need one.'

He smiled slightly. 'Better have two. One might get dropped.'

'Thank you.'

I had turned to go when he said, 'Hold hard. You haven't signed for them.'

'I'm so sorry.' I took out my pen and pulled at the cap but it had stuck.

He offered me a black fountain-pen. 'Try this.'

'Thanks.' It was a very expensive-looking pen and I was surprised at a student owning it, but I thought he was probably in his final year and expecting to qualify shortly. He looked to be in the middle twenties. Perhaps he had brought this pen to boost him through his finals.

I had reached the door when I glanced unthinkingly

at the tubes in my hand. They were marked '*Sodium Citrate*'.

'Oh, dear.' I turned back. 'I'm afraid you have given me the wrong thing. I wanted cilliated tubes.'

His lips twitched but his face was expressionless. 'So you said, Nurse. But I think you'll find those are satisfactory.'

I had no time to argue with students. 'Please, can I have a cilliated one?'

He said gently, 'No.'

The man must be crazy. I pointed out, 'But Sister Victoria said –'

He shook his head. 'She didn't, you know. You must have thought she did. This is what Mrs. Levine always has on Thursdays.'

'Does she?' I was still doubtful. 'Are you sure?'

His lips twitched again. 'Yes, I think I am.' He saw I was not convinced so he added, 'I work up here quite a bit.'

I looked down at the wretched glass tubes. 'And you think these are all right?'

'Look, you run along with those,' he said confidentially. 'If you find you are right and I was wrong and Sister is demanding a cilliated tube, just tell her we haven't got one.'

'Isn't there one in this lab?' I was openly incredulous.

His eyes narrowed. 'Nurse, do you know what a cilliated tube is?'

I said truthfully, 'No, I don't.'

He grinned. 'That makes two of us.'

I looked round the room. 'What about one of the pathologists? Where are they all? Wouldn't they know? Dr. – Dr. –' I tried to recall the name of the head of the Path Lab about whom Sister P.T.S. had lectured us. 'Dr. Loftus. Is he here? In one of those little rooms? Wouldn't he know?'

He said, 'Oh, I doubt that he'd be much good. He wouldn't know either.'

I said I thought that was nonsense. 'Dr. Loftus knows everything.'

He raised an eyebrow. 'Friend of yours, Nurse?'

'Never seen him in my life. But Sister P.T.S. says he's the most brilliant pathologist this place has had for over a century.'

'Even Homer sometimes nods,' he murmured.

'Thank you for your help. I'll tell Sister Victoria what you said.'

He walked to the door with me. 'Take my hint and just hand them to her. Say nothing unless she queries it.' He opened the door. 'It's always a mistake to offer gratuitous information, so I have discovered. Good morning, Nurse.'

When I got back to the ward I saw to my horror that Dr. Thatcher had reached Bed 31 and Mrs. Levine was placidly knitting. But when I arrived beside Sister and tentatively held out the tubes with the label upward, to my heartfelt relief she nodded. 'That's right, Nurse. Put them on the trolley by the door. Dr. Thatcher is coming back to do it after lunch.' She added that I had been absent too long. 'You must not dawdle on errands. Now look sharp and see to your lunch-trolley.'

At one, Sister sent me to my own lunch. 'And on the way, Nurse Shane, will you go along to the laboratory, take back that spare tube and the one Dr. Thatcher has just used, and ask to speak with Dr. Loftus. Will you tell him that Dr. Thatcher will be most obliged if he can come and transfuse Mrs.

Levine this afternoon?'

When I reached the Lab and saw that it was full of men in long white coats and how lucky I had been earlier to find it empty, I was even more thankful. I disregarded the amicable notice on the door and stopped on the threshold. There was a wire cage attached to the wall just inside the door and this was labelled, '*Please leave all test tubes here, Nurses*'. The Lab clearly went in for labels. But there was no notice telling me what to do with my verbal request. I was about to nerve myself to ask the nearest white coat when with a surge of relief I caught sight of the back of a brown head and the one pair of tweed-clad shoulders in that sea of white.

I walked through the crowd of men. You get very used to walking through a crowd of men in hospital, and it is not at all embarrassing since no doctor ever takes the slightest notice of a junior nurse. None of them glanced at me; I might have been invisible, which suited me. My friend of this morning had his back to me. He was standing twirling his glasses in one hand and listening to a small round man whom I actually recognised as the Senior Medical Officer to the hospital. The S.M.O. looked at and through me and went on with what he was saying.

I waited beside them, hoping my student would look round, but he was listening too intently to notice anything. As usual, I was in a hurry. Sister Dining-Room disapproved of probationers arriving late to meals. I coughed slightly, but that had no effect, so in desperation I held my test tubes out in front of his face. That did it. He looked round at once and raised an eyebrow.

'Something I can do for you, Nurse?' he asked civilly.

‘Please.’ I glanced at the S.M.O. and then at a tall, dark, rather elderly man with a clever face who had strolled over to where we stood. This was almost certainly the great Dr. Loftus and I was tongue-tied with shyness.

My student nodded back understandingly. He said, ‘Excuse me,’ to the two other men and moved away from the group. ‘What’s up, Nurse?’

‘Please, which is Dr. Loftus?’ I told him quickly the message I had to give. ‘Sister said I was to ask to speak to him, but I don’t know who to ask.’

He glanced over his shoulder. ‘He’s around here somewhere. I’ll tell him for you.’

‘Will that be all right? He won’t mind getting a request at second hand?’

‘He won’t mind. You leave it to me.’ He smiled faintly. ‘But how about those tubes? Don’t you think you had better leave them with me? You don’t really want to take them back to Victoria.’

I gave them to him. ‘I had forgotten all about them.’ I was a little anxious at the way he shoved both my precious tubes into one of his jacket pockets, but he was being so kind that I did not like to say anything. ‘Thank you very much,’ I risked a smile. ‘I’ll have to rush to lunch. Sister Dining-Room doesn’t like it if we are late.’

‘Then you mustn’t be late,’ he said. ‘Goodbye.’

‘Thank you again,’ I repeated and walked back to the door. The room was as full as ever, but I noticed it was now silent. Several men, who had previously ignored me, now glanced curiously at me. I wondered if I had broken some unwritten rule. Perhaps nurses did not speak to students in Path Labs?

As I closed the door I heard a man say, ‘Friend of yours, Joe?’ and then my student’s voice, ‘An old professional acquaintance from Victoria.' And somebody laughed.

That afternoon was a visiting afternoon and the ward was free of teaching rounds. Because of the nature of her illness, Mrs. Levine was a law unto herself. She had to have regular blood transfusions and she was progressing very satisfactorily.

'But she has to have them on the dot, Shane,' Nurse Astor explained to me. 'Visitors or no visitors. She doesn't mind. Her husband has permission from Sister to come in on Friday instead of today and that suits him better, as Friday is his day off.'

Sister was off until five that evening, and the Staff Nurse had told Nurse Astor to see to the transfusion. 'Take Nurse Shane with you. Show her how to set the trolley and how to chaperon for Dr. Loftus and she can do it next week.'

I followed Nurse Astor into the sterilising room. She took two clean face-masks from the glass jar by the door and threw one at me. 'Put that on, Shane.' She washed her hands, then hitched forward a trolley with her feet. 'Now. This is how you set for a transfusion. Watch and assimilate, my child. Setting for a transfusion is something every nurse should be able to do on her head in her sleep. You never know when you are going to be asked to set one quickly. The only thing you can be certain is that you will be asked. You do it this way.'

When she had finished and made me check aloud what she had placed on the glass trolley-top she covered it with a sterile towel. 'All we now need is old Doc Loftus.'

I was concentrating on the order in which she had laid the instruments. 'Is he very old?' I asked vaguely.

‘Not really.’ She re-tied her mask and her eyes smiled over the top of the white linen square. ‘In fact, not at all. He’s about thirty something.’ She calculated. ‘He was S.M.O. when he was twenty-seven. I know that because that was a record. He was the youngest S.M.O. Mike’s ever had.’

‘How did he manage it, then?’

‘Brains,’ she said briefly. ‘I’ve just been working it out. He’s thirty-six.’ She opened the door that overlooked the corridor and propped it open. ‘We’ll wait here until he comes in.’

I said, ‘Isn’t that rather young for the head of a department?’

She nodded. ‘You are telling me it’s rather young. In fact, he hit another record when he got that job. And with him it’s sheer merit and nothing else. He’s not the ambitious type. Which is rather a pity in some ways,’ she added thoughtfully.

I asked why.

Her eyes considered me. ‘I shouldn’t have said that. You’re a bit too new to join in the hospital gossip, but having said it, I may as well explain, if we’ve got the time.’ She looked down the corridor. ‘Yes, we have. There’s a certain Sister here who is an absolute peach,’ she went on. ‘She works in Luke. She’s quite young. She married when she was a junior and her husband was a Mike’s man.’

I said, ‘Was?’

She nodded. ‘That’s right. He was killed in an accident. Nice man, they say. A great friend of old Joe’s. And Rosemary Lockhart – that’s Sister Luke to the likes of us – is another great friend of Joe’s. And we’ve all rather hoped that something might come of that friendship. They’d make a good pair, and according to rumour, Joe Loftus was always fond of her when she was a junior and he a student. But Alistair Lockhart moved in and that was the end of things for Joe. Then, of course, it all changed. Naturally, Joe was not going to rush things. As I've just told you, he's not that type.'

A faint, unpleasant prickling had been going on under my cap for the last few minutes. 'What – er – what does Dr. Loftus look like, Nurse?'

Her eyes danced. 'What are you expecting him to look like, Shane?'

I hesitated. 'Sort of elderly, clever, with glasses and a stoop, and ash on his waistcoat.' I was describing the dark man who had appeared during my last few seconds in the Lab this morning and hoping that I was right.

'You are in for a shock, my child,' she announced cheerfully. 'You are describing the perfect stage pathologist. The only man we have got who looks anything like your description is Dr. Stranger, the tropical fevers man. The bunch in the Path Lab look more like the forward line of our Rugger fifteen, which is hardly surprising since most of them have figured in it at one time or other.'

I could have told her that I had already had my shock, but instead I asked how many doctors worked in the Lab.

'You call them pathologists, Shane,' she said kindly. 'Not doctors, although of course they are. The doctors are the physicians, understand?'

I nodded. 'I can't say exactly how many,' she went on, 'but it's quite a bunch. Nice lot, too, and different.'

'What do you mean?'

'Well, they are part of Mike's and work in the wards, but they are a race apart. Not quite of this world. They are all almost frighteningly clever, only they are so civil that we tend to forget it. They never fuss or stand on any etiquette at all, which is most refreshing to us hard-working nurses. But you were right about one thing – at least, where Joe is concerned.'

I said, 'What's that, Nurse?'

Her eyes were smiling, 'Absent-minded. When that man has a problem on tap, he's apt to forget everything and everybody, including his glasses and his car. He once was in the middle of the Strand working out something in his head to while away the odd half-hour in a traffic-jam. Apparently he got the answer and realised that it was something the boys in the Lab ought to know at once, so he got out of the car and walked to the nearest telephone-box.'

'Leaving the car in the middle of the Strand?' I was so fascinated that I forgot my own confusion.

'Leaving the car in the middle of the Strand. By a stroke of luck it was up against the pavement. This was before they brought in the new parking rules so nobody bothered too much about that. But there was a terrific flap on next morning because the porter who keeps an eye on the men's cars thought it had been stolen. He rushed up to the Path Lab in a panic and broke the news to Joe Loftus. Joe took it all very calmly and then said it was probably still sitting in the middle of the Strand as he had taken a taxi back to the hospital on leaving the telephone-box and the car had somehow slipped his memory.'

'Does he often do things like that, Nurse?'

'Not often.' She sounded regretful. 'But once in a while and then we remember he's human. Otherwise, although a good soul, he's inclined to be inhuman. He would obviously so much rather look down a microscope than do anything else.'

'What about Sister Luke?' Was it conceivable that we were discussing the same man? That man I had thought a student this morning had been far too kind to be ever called inhuman.

'Sister Luke is the one person who has ever been able to break through the dividing line. He and she have been friends for years and she isn't unduly impressed by the collection of letters after his name. But to her I imagine he's her old pal Joe, and she is not a high-powered frilly-capped Sister, but just Rosemary Fildes who married his greatest friend. And there's another thing, she must know he's in love with her. We all know that. So naturally when she's around he's a different man. But with the rest of us –' she shrugged – 'he's very civil and we all like him, but we all know he forgets our existences as frequently as he forgets his glasses – which is approximately a dozen times a day!'

Nurse Astor glanced down the corridor again and this time she took hold of the trolley. 'Here we go,' she murmured, then more loudly, 'Good afternoon, Dr. Loftus. Mrs. Levine is all ready for you.'

He said, 'Good afternoon, Nurse Astor. Thank you.' He glanced my way.

Astor said, 'Do you object to Nurse Shane coming to watch? The Staff Nurse thought it might be a good opportunity for Nurse to find out about these things.'

His eyes rested coolly on my masked face and I was very grateful for that mask. I wondered how I had ever mistaken this tall, bespectacled, serious-faced man for a student. He seemed years older than he had this morning, and the change was not only due to his long white coat. 'I agree with your Staff Nurse,' he said. 'I think it would be a sound scheme for Nurse

Shane to find out about these things.'

I said, 'Yes, Dr. Loftus,' feeling about eight years old and two inches high. He did not answer but waited politely for us to precede him up the ward. By the time we reached Bed No. 32 I was acutely miserable. I knew I was being absurd, that he was also a little responsible for my folly because he had let me go on thinking he was a student, but that did not make me any happier.

He vanished to one of the sinks to wash. Nurse Astor, who was chatting with Mrs. Levine, turned to me. 'Hang around outside the curtains, Nurse, and see that none of the visitors bang into Dr. Loftus when he has his hands scrubbed. You don't have to do anything but direct the traffic, if any.'

I did as she said. The visitors glanced incuriously at myself and went on with their conversations. When he had washed for five minutes he came back to the curtains. His sleeves were rolled high and his arms and hands were dripping. 'Would you mind holding that curtain back for me, Nurse Shane? I'm afraid I can't touch it myself.'

'I'm sorry.' Stupidly I had forgotten this point.

He said very quietly, 'Found any cilliated tubes yet, Nurse?' His voice was formal and he was now wearing a mask so I could not see his expression. But his eyes were laughing, not at me, but with me.

I was too embarrassed to do anything but shake my head and pull back the curtain.

When he had finished and left the ward, I was sent back to my duties. For no good reason all my gloom had disappeared. I hummed quietly to myself although outside the window I could see that the afternoon had turned to grey as summer afternoons so often do in London. I felt as if a small private sun of my own was shining on me. And then I took a mental grip on my thoughts and remembered Sister Luke, whom Astor had described as a perfect peach. The sun went down and the bathroom became as grey as the sky outside the window.

Christine Blake sailed into the music-room in the Nurses' Home one afternoon a few weeks later and found me at the piano. 'Alice, you aren't still playing that piano! What a way to spend a day off.'

I sat back on the stool and smiled at her. 'But I like spending a day off this way.'

She flopped down on one of the comfortable leather armchairs and said she did not think it was natural. 'Here you are, a fine young woman of twenty, and you spend all your off-time reading good books, sewing, and pounding that wretched instrument. Not that you don't pound it well. You do. But, Alice, a girl needs some fun and games and light relief at this job.'

Chris was a high-spirited girl. She was also very good-looking. She was tall and fair, and had enormous brown eyes and dark brown eyebrows that were natural and very striking against her near-flaxen hair. My first reaction on seeing her in the Preliminary Training School had been to wonder what a girl like her was doing taking up nursing. I later discovered the simple answer was that she wanted to be a nurse. But she managed to fit in a very complicated social life despite the long, full hours we worked in the wards and the many lectures that junior nurses have to attend. Chris was a Londoner and had a large circle of friends, most of whom seemed to be young men, outside the hospital. She was very kind to me and was always suggesting that I joined the various parties or visited her home for my day off. My own home was in Hampshire, and although I would have loved to go there for my weekly day off, my finances ruled that out and I could only manage the fare once a month. I missed my parents and home, but I did not mind being alone or spending my days off in the manner that so shocked Chris.

She got up and leant against the piano. 'Alice, I wish you'd come out with Alec and me tonight. Alec can easily raise another man, and it would be fun.'

'It might be indeed, but not for me. No, thank you very much, but I prefer my piano.'

She obviously did not believe me. 'My dear Alice, you can't. You must want a change.'

'But it is a change,' I assured her. 'Listen.' I had explained all this to her on previous occasions when she had kindly tried to drag me out, but I thought I had better tell her again. 'I'm not used to gallivanting like you are, Chris, and I'm certainly not used to hordes of young men, or even one young man.'

'You've got a brother. Surely you knew his friends?'

I agreed that I had a brother. 'But Mark is nine years older than I am, and although that doesn't make much difference now, when we were growing up it did. And, anyway, he's in the Navy and like all sailors he's always at sea on the other side of the world, and his friends are sailing with him.'

She propped her lovely face on her hands. 'Your father is a parson. Parsons always know everyone in the village.'

'We do know everyone in our village, and all the surrounding villages, both of them! But that doesn't mean that we know masses of the sort of people you are talking about. And we have a lot of fun at home, but it's rather different fun from what you have up here.'

'Jumble sales? Whist-drives? Garden fêtes? You can't call those fun, Ally.'

'Which shows how little you know of country life,' I said. 'Jumble sales are the maddest things I know. My mother and I, and all our helpers love them. They are an absolute free for all, and jolly good value, too,' I added reminiscently.

She shook her head. 'I don't get it. How about parties, dances, things like that?'

I grinned. 'I once went to a Hunt Ball with a couple of cousins and loathed every minute of it. Not the Ball itself, that was all right, but the fact that I did not know anybody. My cousins were bored stiff because my aunt had said they had to take me, and I counted the hours until it was over. It was an awful lot of hours, too.'

'Is that the only dance you've ever been to?'

'The only dance that you'd call a dance. I've been to various socials at home when we've had dancing, but they were just friendly gatherings, no one dressed up or anything.'

Chris shook her head again and said she thought it was all too grim for words. 'Haven't you met anyone you'd like to go out with?'

I looked at the keyboard. 'I told you our village doesn't go in for surplus young men,' I said evasively.

Home Sister opened the music-room door at that moment.

'Is Nurse Blake in here? Nurse, you are wanted on the external telephone.'

I sighed with relief when Chris followed Sister out. I did not want to lie and yet I could not possibly admit to her what I hardly dared to admit to myself. It was such a foolish admission. I had seen one man, and I still saw glimpses of him from time to time when he had occasion to come to Victoria or in the hospital corridors. But apart from that one day he had never spoken to me again, or looked as if he recollected who I was. I was sure he did not. What reason had he to remember me, apart from my mistake? Even that was hardly sufficient to imprint a person like myself on a man's mind.

I had no delusions about my face or my character. There is nothing, I thought with a slight smile, like an elder brother's comments for ridding a girl of delusions or conceit. None of the many young men I had seen around Victoria had troubled to give me a second glance, and I had not expected them to do so. I had also enjoyed watching the impact of Chris on the Medical School. As a junior nurse she was technically beneath anyone's notice, but I had been very amused at the turning of heads and the amount of questions the students found it necessary to ask, coming into the sluice or bathrooms when she was around because they just had to know the answer. One had even asked us the time, with the large ward clock striking as he asked.

I smiled again as I went on playing. I was no Chris and that was all there was to it. And there was also this Sister Luke of whom I was hearing a good deal from my fellow pros in Luke. I had yet to see her; but I knew she was a legend in her own working life and the general opinion was that, as Nurse Astor had said, she was a perfect peach.

# BOOKS BY LUCILLA ANDREWS

*The Golden Hour*, and all of the other novels written by Lucilla Andrews, will be released as paperbacks by Wyndham Books, exclusively on Amazon. Ebook editions of all of Lucilla's books are already available.

To be the first to know when new paperbacks are published, and to learn about special offers and news, sign up to the free Lucilla Andrews newsletter on the official website at **www.lucillaandrews.com**

Printed in Great Britain
by Amazon

49341367R00117